the Grapevine

For information, please contact:
Wings Publishing
11144 Valeside Crescent
Carmel, Indiana 46032
thegrapevinebook@att.net

Printed and bound in the United States.
First printing 2012.

ISBN 978-0-9886686-0-7

Cover and book design by Saxon Design Inc.

the Grapevine

Berkley Duck

Wings Publishing

1

The chairwoman of the symphony orchestra board of trustees sat opposite my desk. She crossed her shapely legs and smiled, unleashing the charm that had separated substantial chunks of hard-earned – or inherited – wealth from many of our mutual friends. Her powers of persuasion were legendary, and whatever success the symphony was having in its current fundraising efforts was largely attributable to her skills and contacts in the community. She wasn't just a pretty face, however. I had heard that she ran the board with an iron hand. I was fairly certain that she wasn't here to thank me for my financial support, which had never been sufficient to attract attention at such a high level.

"Wonderful to see you again, Alex," she said, with apparent sincerity. Our relationship had consisted of a mix of always pleasant, but never intensive, social and civic encounters.

"Good to see you, too, Susannah," I replied. "How's Morrie? How's the family?" Morris Townsend, Susannah's husband, had been a sometime client of my former law firm. We were only casually acquainted, but I had answered questions from his staff on several occasions. In addition – or perhaps as a supplement – to his career as a successful real estate developer, he was active behind the scenes in local politics and spread a lot of money around where it would do the most good. Despite the market crunch, Morrie seemed to be doing just fine.

"He's just fine," Susannah confirmed. She went on to brief me on the activities of their three children. The eldest son was in his second year at the well-regarded medical school downstate and the middle child, a girl, had just entered as a freshman at an Ivy League university. The youngest, another boy, was still in high school.

After some additional catching up on mutual friends, she came to the point of her visit. "I need your help," she said, "on a rather sensitive matter."

My specialty is tax law, but my background was in for-profit work. Most of my clients are businesses and individuals that have interesting relationships with state and federal taxing authorities. I explained to Susannah that I didn't know all that much about the rules regarding the operation of non-profits.

"This isn't about taxes," she replied, shifting position in her chair and looking away. For a few moments she studied the Winslow Homer print on the wall next to my desk, a gift from my daughter, nicely framed, and then turned back to me. She looked me straight in the eye.

"Can I trust you to keep what I tell you confidential?" she asked.

"Certainly," I said.

She held my gaze for a few moments more. "I think someone is embezzling from the symphony," she then said. We sat quietly for a few moments as I considered this news. The symphony was highly rated for its artistry, not in the top rank but of excellent quality for a city of our size. But, as was happening elsewhere, the symphony had slipped into a pattern of recurring deficits despite the heroic fund-raising efforts of Susannah and her co-trustees, and the problem was steadily worsening. Ticket sales covered a share of the orchestra's expenses, but it depended on its endowment, and even more so on contributions, to stay in business. The contributors included the usual mix of local businesses, wealthy patrons, less well-to-do fans of classical music and a large number of donors who gave a couple of hundred dollars a year because they thought the symphony was a cultural asset for the city. But the big money came from a small number of private foundations and from local tax revenues channeled to the orchestra by the city through an arts council. None of the general public, the boards of directors and staffs of the major contributors, or the elected officials responsible for tax revenues, would react favorably to the news that money they had given to the orchestra had been allowed to slip into the hands of a malefactor. I could see the need to keep this revelation private. Disclosure would trigger a public relations disaster and threaten the orchestra's continued existence.

"For obvious reasons," Susannah went on," I've kept this very quiet. I've only discussed it with two people. One is our treasurer, Ellis Kirkland." I knew of Ellis Kirkland, but we were not acquainted. She was a vice president of some kind in the complex hierarchy of the city's largest independent bank.

"I've known Ellis for years and I respect her integrity and her judgment," Susannah continued. "She said we would have to tell our public accountants what I had learned. She pointed out that they will begin their annual audit of our year-end financial statements in a few weeks, and they'll ask us whether we are aware of any evidence of fraud. She also thought that there was a good chance that the audit would uncover the theft, and maybe the thief. I asked her not to say anything to the accountants just yet. She agreed that we could wait.

"Also," she added, "I have consulted with Harvey Anderson." I knew Harvey Anderson. He was a middle-aged partner in one of my old firm's competitors. If we had a silk stocking law firm in town, it was Harvey's. Harvey himself was a graduate of an Ivy League college and its law school. Although he concentrated his practice in trusts and estates, he and I both had been involved in matters in which our respective clients were attempting to put together business deals. We were members of the same country club, where I frequently saw him entertaining clients and, more often, potential clients. He was a smart lawyer, but I thought that both his client advice and his business development tactics were pretty aggressive. We got along, but I wouldn't say we were friends. He had taken over as the symphony's outside lawyer three years ago following the retirement of his mentor, who had acted in that role for many years.

"He suggested, under the circumstances, that I talk to you," Susannah said.

The circumstances in question were to become clear in short order, but my first reaction was mild surprise that I had been on Harvey's radar in this context. I was of the impression that he didn't consider me to be in his league. I briefly contemplated asking Susannah whether Harvey had advised her to report what she knew to the police, but decided against it. Whatever advice Harvey had given her, it was probably a lawyer-client privileged communication, and regardless of what Susannah had been told, here she was, sitting in my office, asking for my help. I rephrased the question.

"What did Harvey think I could do for you?"

"I'm not comfortable sitting around waiting for the auditors," she answered, "and based on what I've learned I'm not sure they're going to solve our problem. I think there's more to this than someone cooking the books. I need someone who can look into what I have, determine for certain what, if anything, has gone wrong and report back to me. Harvey told me about your background with the FBI, and it seemed to me that you were a good choice. I don't want to bring in a private detective, and I don't want to report this to our insurance carrier until I know the facts. You hear so many things through the grapevine."

I contemplated the length and breadth of the grapevine in which Susannah was likely to be a participant and nodded my agreement. "If there is a problem," she went on, "and if we can fix it without involving the police, we'll do so and then report our findings to the board of trustees. If a crime has been committed, then we'll give what we know to the authorities and we can manage the handling of the insurance claim. But I don't want a team of lawyers traipsing into the office and I want this done now, not in a month or six weeks. We thought that you had the experience and the discretion to handle this the right way."

She hesitated, then continued. "Also, we – that is, I – thought… well, hoped…that your fees might be less than what Harvey said it would cost if his firm did the work." Harvey's firm had a reputation for thorough work, abundant staffing of assignments and high hourly rates, and it was probable that his fee estimate had sent her scrambling for a more affordable option.

It occurred to me that Harvey's suggestion that Susannah contact me probably was influenced by his judgment that I wasn't going to supplant him as the symphony's legal advisor, even if I dazzled Susannah with my skills. My firm, Carrolton Associates, is a small operation. I'm Carrolton, and I have three partners, each of whom also had come from a large firm. Their backgrounds are in environmental law, health care and governmental relations. We have office space and a conference room in one of the older downtown buildings, and a small staff. We try to keep the firm informal and to not take ourselves too seriously. We see the practice as a way to keep our hands in the game, which we all enjoy, and it provides sufficient income to make it worth the effort while leaving time for other interests. We aren't really in this for the money, as each of us left our previous employments with sufficient resources to maintain our comfortable, although not affluent, lifestyles.

I managed to suppress my reaction to the disclosure that I was a low cost alternative to what Susannah probably regarded as her "A" team. She leaned forward in her chair. "Let me say again that this is extremely sensitive. The only people who know about it are Ellis and I – and, of course, Harvey, and I've told him that he is to keep this information strictly confidential. I don't want this to get around. I haven't even told John Martin." Martin was the symphony's chief executive officer. "I'm hoping," Susannah concluded, "that you can get on this right away and sort it out in the next few days, so I'll know where we stand."

"Well," I answered, thinking out loud. "I wouldn't need to review any accounting records or your internal procedures. Your auditors will do that. But I'm not clear what else can be done. How can I be of any help if I can't talk to your people?"

"Are you willing to do this for me or not?" she asked. She had lost some of her composure and now seemed a little on edge. "If you are, and if we can agree on a timetable and what it's going to cost, then I'll show you what I have and we'll take it from there."

I leaned back and thought. I was intrigued. I enjoyed investigative work, but I hadn't done much since my FBI days. I liked Susannah and sympathized with her situation. In my previous life I had worked on several embezzlement cases and I knew how embezzlers operated. I didn't have anything on my plate that couldn't be put aside for a few days. I guess I was a little flattered that Susannah had come to me with a matter of such importance to her and to the community, even if I was her second choice. And I was curious to find out what she had discovered. I told her I was in. I quoted an hourly rate, with a small retainer and not-to-exceed cap, that I thought would cover our overhead and provide a small profit, assuming that my report could be completed and in her hands within ten days.

Susannah seemed relieved. She agreed to my terms and thought the timetable was reasonable. She pulled a checkbook from her purse and wrote a personal check for the retainer. She said that I was to provide her with an itemized statement at the conclusion of the engagement. Depending on the outcome, she would then consider whether to present my bill to the symphony for reimbursement. In the meantime, I was to consider her as my client.

She then asked if I could meet at her home at three o'clock that afternoon to review what she had uncovered. I said I could.

When I got there, Susannah was dead.

2

The home of Susannah and Morris Townsend was located in an exclusive suburb on the north side of the metropolitan area. I pulled my car into the circular driveway and parked at the front door. It was twelve minutes past three o'clock, I noted on the dashboard's digital readout. I had been delayed by a construction project on the parkway. There was another car parked farther up the drive, a white sedan.

It was a pleasant late summer day following a long period of hot, humid weather. I got out of the car, crunched across the brilliant white gravel, unmarred by a single weed or blade of grass, and walked across the porch to the door. Apparently the air conditioning had been turned off because some of the windows and the front door were open. I could see into the hallway through the screen door, although the interior was dark against the bright outside light. I was about to ring the bell when, my eyes adjusting to the light inside, I thought I could see someone lying at the far end of the hallway.

"Susannah?" I called through the door. No answer. I rang the bell, but there was no response. Now alarmed, I tried the door knob, and it opened. I put down my briefcase and hurried down the hall. I didn't like what I found.

Susannah was laying face-down, fully clothed in the business suit she had been wearing that morning. Her head and shoulders extended into the front hallway and the rest of her body was in a small entry that led from the main hall to the kitchen. Her arms were at her side. A kitchen knife, a big one, was lodged in her back, right above her heart. There was a great deal of blood, and it looked disturbingly fresh.

I staggered backward. My stomach lurched and I thought for a moment that I might pass out. I had never seen a dead body before, other than in a funeral home, and none of them looked like Susannah. I don't consider myself a tough guy, and this was way beyond anything in my prior experience. Pulling myself together, I reached into my pocket and retrieved my cell phone. I was about to dial 911 when it occurred to me that I was standing at the scene of a murder – a very recent murder, to all appearances – and I had no idea where the killer was.

I froze, now listening intently and looking around. I couldn't see anything other than a limited view into the kitchen and back up the hallway through which I had arrived. I noticed, for the first time, that I had passed several other openings and doorways off the hall between the front door and where I now stood. In the opposite direction, the hallway terminated, a few feet away, at double glass doors that led onto a patio. I remembered that I had called out Susannah's name and rung the bell, so if anyone else was in the house, he – or she – knew I was there. Other than for the chirping of cicadas outside a kitchen window, it was dead quiet.

I didn't like the idea of walking back up the hallway, past all those other rooms. I put my phone back in my pocket and moved as quietly as I could to the double glass doors. I tried the handle. It turned, but the lock was dead-bolted and wouldn't open without a key. The glass window panes and mullions looked substantial. They were probably designed to keep someone from breaking in, and I doubted that I could break out. I certainly wasn't going to squeeze my way past Susannah, walking through all that blood, in the hope that there might be some other exit through the kitchen. For all I knew, the killer was crouching behind the island that I could see in the middle of the room.

Just then I heard a creaking noise from somewhere inside the house. I immediately thought of all those times when, alone at home, I had heard a strange noise and was sure that someone else was inside, but it was only the normal sounds of the floors or ductwork warming or cooling. Was that what I had just heard, or something more sinister? I decided that I had to move, and the hallway was the only way out. I looked around for some kind of a weapon, but the only thing I saw was the knife sticking out of Susannah's back. I wasn't going to touch that.

I started back up the hallway, staying on the right hand side where there were fewer access points. A staircase ran up from ground level to my right, nearer the front door. I passed the first door on the left, which seemed to be the entry to the master bedroom suite. I couldn't see anyone inside. I passed a closed door on my right. I was nearing the staircase. There was another door on my left. I turned and looked up the stairs, seeing nothing. I started across the open space between the stairs and the front door, heard a sudden noise behind me, felt a gentle rush of air, and then everything went black.

In my next brush with reality, I found myself staring up at people I didn't know, who were going in and out of focus. My head hurt. I tried to lift my arm to examine my head but couldn't. A voice said, "He's coming to." As my vision cleared, I saw an emergency medical technician kneeling beside me, ministering to a wound on my head. On the opposite side was a cop. He didn't look so helpful.

After a few minutes, the tech said, "I think you can sit up now. Go slow." He helped me into a sitting position, with my back against the wall. "OK?" he asked. I mumbled something affirmative. He shined a light in my eyes and asked me what day it was. He said I might have had a concussion and I should check with my doctor, then packed up his gear and left. My wrists were in front of me, in handcuffs. I stared at them, trying put together what had happened. It came to me where I was and what I had discovered in the kitchen entry. There were several people down the main hall in that direction, clustered around what I assumed was Susannah's body. Then I saw that my hands were covered with blood. I knew that head wounds bled a lot, but why was it on my hands?

The cop signaled to another man down the hall, and he walked over to where I was sitting. He was an African-American, in plain clothes, but a police ID badge hung from his jacket pocket. He crouched down, so that we were face-to-face. The name plate on the badge holder said "Lieutenant R. Hammond."

"Your name?" he asked.

It took a couple of tries before I could get it out. "Alex Carrolton," I said.

"Good answer," he said. "That's what it says on your driver's license. Care to tell me what you are doing here, Mr. Carrolton?"

"Somebody hit me on the head," I said.

"I didn't mean why are you sitting on the floor; I meant, what are you doing in this house?"

"I had an appointment with Susannah Townsend," I said. "Three o'clock."

"So she was alive when you got here." He stated it as a fact, not a question.

My mind suddenly became a lot clearer. "No, no!" I said. I told him the circumstances of my arrival at the house, how I found Susannah's body, my attempt to leave and my supposition that Susannah's killer also had attacked me. "Why am I handcuffed?" I asked.

"Well," said Lieutenant Hammond, "we think that's Mrs. Townsend's blood on your hands, and we found this next to you on the floor." He held up a plastic bag containing a bloody knife that bore a distressing resemblance to the one I saw sticking out of Susannah's back.

"Are we going to find your fingerprints on the handle?" he inquired, politely.

3

The next 24 hours were not the worst of my life, but they certainly could have been. Things got headed in the right direction when, upon my arrival at the central police station, downtown, my one telephone call succeeded in reaching Jerry Marsdon, one of my former law partners. Jerry had some experience with criminal cases. As I had requested, he had called Tommy Glynn.

Tommy was a retiree from the metropolitan police force, a beat cop who had advanced to the level of lieutenant before retiring on partial disability after being badly injured in a shoot-out while investigating a domestic dispute. In that incident, Tommy probably saved the life of the niece of one of our partners. Carrolton Associates kept him on a modest retainer that supplemented his pension and gave us access to his expertise when we needed it. Our clients don't often find themselves involved with law enforcement, but it happens. And now it had happened to me. Since bringing him on board, Tommy and I had become pretty close. We enjoyed each other's company and I valued his judgment and perspective. Jerry and Tommy showed up at the station within ten minutes of each other, about 45 minutes later.

By now it was early evening. Tommy started making the rounds, talking to any of his old buddies who were available. Jerry joined me in a small interview room where I had been sitting, alone. I had been read my rights, allowed to clean up my hands, and fingerprinted. I also had been given a sandwich from a vending machine, a soft drink and some aspirin for what was now a pounding headache. It wasn't helping. I told Jerry my story, and he seemed comfortable with what I had to say. We agreed that I should give a formal statement to the police. Jerry stepped out and returned a few minutes later with Lieutenant Hammond, who had a slick digital recorder about the size of a pack of cigarettes. I went through the whole thing again, on the record, mostly answering questions from Hammond. He seemed particularly interested in the white sedan I had seen parked in the Townsend's driveway. Unfortunately, I hadn't paid it any attention and couldn't even tell him the brand, let alone a license number. He and Jerry left the room.

When Jerry returned about twenty minutes later, he looked relieved.

"Good news," he announced. "I think I can beat the death penalty."

"Very funny," I said. Jerry had an odd sense of humor.

"Seriously," he went on, "my firm impression is that Hammond doesn't think you had anything to do with this. I also talked to Tommy. He says the police don't have any motive so far and, based on what you've told me, they aren't going to find one. They have no explanation for why you were found unconscious on the floor, other than the reason you gave them, and they understand that the blood and the knife could have been planted on you after you were knocked out. There was no other car in the driveway when the police arrived, so they have to consider the possibility that someone drove off after attacking you. Also, Morris Townsend confirmed that you had an appointment with his wife for this afternoon."

"So can I leave?"

"Probably not until sometime tomorrow. They need to do forensics on the knife and the blood to see if they find anything inconsistent with your version of what happened, and their techs are still at the scene collecting evidence. Assuming nothing new pops up that points in your direction, you should be out of here by the end of the day."

"Great. And in the meantime the TV stations and the newspaper are busy trashing my reputation."

"As far as I know," Jerry said, "your name hasn't come up, only that the police are 'questioning witnesses.'" He made little quotation marks in the air. "And Tommy is on that. He called your partner – Ed somebody?"

"Ed Wilson." Ed was our governmental relations expert and knew how to handle the media.

"Yeah, Ed Wilson. Tommy says Ed is talking with the public affairs officer about how we'd like to handle this, and the cops seem to be willing to let Ed take the lead assuming they don't find any reason to hold you. He'll put together a story line that paints you as an innocent bystander – another victim, in fact – in this brutal and senseless attack on one of your personal friends. Wrong place at the wrong time. Lucky to have avoided being killed yourself. Taken into police custody merely as a matter of procedure. Fully cooperating in the investigation. Et cetera. Tommy says Ed is confident this will work, it being the truth and all."

I was beginning to feel better, despite the pain in my head.

"How'd they find me?" I asked.

"Apparently the UPS guy came to the front door with a package, saw you on the floor, and called 911," he said.

"One more question. Could you have Tommy call Laura now, before anything hits the news? He has the number." Laura was my ex-wife. We had parted four years ago, on as good terms as anyone could hope for under the circumstances. Neither of us had done anything to make the other mad enough to hold a grudge; we just didn't belong together any longer and we both knew it. Our daughter and only child, Rebecca – Becky – had just turned twenty and was a junior at a west coast college. She was the apple of our eyes.

"Sure," said Jerry. "Well, if my not inexpensive legal services are no longer needed here, I'll be on my way." He hesitated at the door. "Oh, and by way, if you drop the soap…"

"Cut it out, Jerry," I interjected. This wasn't the time for prison humor.

He smiled anyway. "Have a nice night," he said, and walked out. I hoped he was kidding about his fee; we were ex-partners after all. But with Jerry you never knew.

I was led to a holding cell. Fortunately, other than for a violent murder in one of the city's nicest residential areas, it had been a quiet day. There were only two other occupants in my quarters. Both were pretty far gone and smelled like a distillery. Had they been conscious and aware of why I was there, they probably would have been more scared of me than I of them. They didn't look like they were going to cause any trouble for several hours at least. I climbed onto a cot attached to the wall, as far away from my roommates as possible, and tried to relax.

But my mind wouldn't stop replaying the events of the day. I tried to quiet the random thoughts by isolating on the key question presented by what had happened over the past twelve hours. Why was Susannah Townsend dead? Attractive, smart, talented, generous, and a pillar of the community in the best possible sense. Why would anyone want to kill her? I couldn't think of anything other than the usual crime novel motives.

Had she been unfaithful to her husband, who stabbed her in a jealous rage? Or maybe it was the other way around: her lover had killed her because she had dumped him in order to go back to Morrie. That premise didn't have much traction. Susannah had a spotless reputation. She emitted a kind of jerk repellant that deflected incoming radar. I myself had sensed this, I had to admit, whenever the obvious advantages of a liaison with her had flitted across my consciousness. To all appearances, she was very happy with Morrie. The lover hypothesis didn't feel right, so I set it aside, at least for the time being.

A variation on this theme occurred to me. Maybe Morrie had lost interest in Susannah, had found someone younger and had decided to eliminate a barrier to future happiness with his new cutie. No fuss, only a little muss, no property settlement and no divorce lawyers to pay. He wouldn't even have to dirty his hands. There were people around town, or so Tommy had once told me, who took on such work for a price, and Morrie probably could get access to them. This seemed unlikely, based on what I knew. Morrie seemed like a stand-up guy, but I couldn't discard this theory outright. I would talk to Tommy about it when I got out.

A revenge killing? But revenge for what? As far as I knew, Susannah wasn't a player in any high stakes intrigues. She had her charity work and her family, but that was about it. I doubted that, over the course of her whole life, she had done damage to anyone on a scale that would trigger the outcome I saw on the floor of her home. On the other hand, there was Morrie. Now here was a possibility. Maybe someone was trying to get to Morrie through Susannah. Morrie had a reputation as a no-holds-barred businessman who, I knew for a fact, had made some enemies on his way to wealth and power. Maybe he had made someone – a competitor, a client, a broker, a contractor, a seller he had taken advantage of, or even a political adversary – angry enough to take out his frustration and anger on Susannah. I filed this one away for further thought.

Maybe the killer's motive wasn't to be found in a crime novel. Maybe it was a random act of violence, a home invasion gone wrong. That seemed possible. Although the Townsend home was in a quiet part of town, crime was everywhere these days. Someone could have been driving by, seen the open door and windows, and decided to try his luck. Poor Susannah comes into the kitchen from the master bedroom, surprises the intruder, she turns to run, he panics, grabs the knife and…I didn't want to visualize the rest.

Maybe it was a family problem. I had heard from my daughter, a couple of years ago, that Susannah's youngest, a boy now about seventeen, had fallen in with a rough crowd at school and gotten into drugs. Susannah hadn't mentioned anything about this during our chit-chat this morning, but why would she air that laundry in a casual conversation with me? Maybe the kid had snapped and killed his mother in a drug-fueled rage. Sad to think about, but I made a mental note to follow up on this also.

I was getting sleepy and my head and body ached with the accumulated stress and abuse of the day. Of course, I thought, the police are pursuing all of these possibilities, and probably more, in their investigation. Finding Susannah's killer didn't fall within my job description and I didn't want to be involved. What I knew, or hypothecated, about Susannah's death wasn't going to find her assailant. I could leave that to the police.

But there was one thing neither the police nor Jerry knew, because I hadn't told them. They didn't know why I was at her home.

4

"Obstruction of justice" has an ugly ring to it, even if it can be argued to be a white collar crime, and I wasn't comfortable with my lack of complete candor with Lieutenant Hammond. Maybe I was still suffering from the effects of the blow to my head and wasn't thinking clearly when he took my statement. That might work as a mitigation plea at my sentencing. But it didn't change the fact that my head was clear now, some twenty hours later, and I hadn't picked up the phone to call headquarters and supplement my statement. Resorting to the distinction-making skills that I had acquired in law school, I rationalized that Lieutenant Hammond hadn't asked me the right question.

When we got to why I was at Susannah's house, I told him that she had asked for my advice on a legal matter. I said, truthfully, that I didn't know the factual background of the problem, which Susannah was going to tell me about. I may have put this in such a way that he concluded that this was all I knew – that Susannah had a legal question. He had asked about my business and how I earned a living, so he knew about my background as a tax lawyer. He probably assumed that I was being called on for tax advice. I didn't disabuse him.

So while I might be able to put up a defense at my trial that could convince, or at least confuse, a jury, I worried that I might be withholding a fact – possible embezzlement at the symphony – that the police would consider important in their investigation. I didn't want anything to stand in the way of the capture and conviction of Susannah's killer. But Susannah herself had been uncertain as to what, if anything, had happened, and she had made it very clear that she considered the public disclosure of a possible theft as a disaster for the orchestra. She had extracted a specific confidentiality commitment from me in my capacity as her lawyer in this matter. The law in our state, as best I could remember it, was that her death did not release me from that pledge. But even if it did, I still didn't feel free to report this element of our conversation even to the police, given Susannah's concern about the grapevine.

From the time I arrived at police headquarters, there was in the back of my mind the thought that I still might be able to do what Susannah had hired me to do: find out if there had been an embezzlement or some other theft, assess how to handle it, and report my findings – if not to her, then to someone else on the symphony's board of trustees. Susannah believed that I could complete my work in a few days. If I could do so, then I could dump the whole mess – if there was one – in the trustees' collective laps and walk away from the problem.

However, I was not entirely clear of police interest. The blood on my hands was Susannah's, my fingerprints were on the knife, and the knife was the murder weapon. Lieutenant R. Hammond had conveyed this information to me upon my release from custody that morning. While conceding that knife probably had been placed in my unconscious hand, he said that I was not to leave town without telling him where I was going. He gave me his card. It turned out that his first name was Ray.

My car had been towed to the police impound, from where I was able to retrieve it. It looked as though it had received a thorough going-over. My briefcase, which contained only a legal pad and my calendar, was in the back seat. I had arrived home a little before noon. I owned a condominium in a rehabilitated warehouse building in the near downtown area. Nice place, fifth floor with a view of the skyline, living room, kitchen, dining alcove, two bedrooms, a study and a small balcony carved out of one corner of the building. I lived there with my cat, Bruno, a big male of uncertain origins that I elected to call a "domestic shorthair." It sounded classier than "alley cat." I found him when he was a kitten on a very cold winter morning in the parking garage next to my office building and brought him home.

I took a shower and lay down on my bed. I hadn't slept much the night before and went out like a light. I woke up about two in the afternoon and fixed a late brunch, an omelet, some fruit, a blueberry muffin and black coffee, and ate it standing at the counter. I took a coffee refill into my study. Sitting in my favorite chair, I tried to think things through. The chair, a recliner, had been with me for years and was beginning to drop small parts onto the carpet from time to time. When it finally gave up, it would be the end of life as I knew it.

I had two separate but related problems if I was going to do anything other than pick up the phone, call Hammond and tell him that I had just remembered that Susannah had mentioned the word "embezzlement." First, there was the risk that the police would uncover that she had, in fact, talked to me about it, and then I would have to explain why I had misled the investigators. I was doubtful that they would graciously accept my plea of attorney-client privilege. Had I made that claim at the time, they probably would have had me up before a judge with a request that he order me to tell them what I knew.

Or, following up on my report that Susannah had consulted with me about a legal matter, they might call Harvey Anderson to see if it had anything to do with the symphony. He had sent Susannah in my direction. What would he say about why she was talking to me? What would he say about her legal problem? How much did he know? Thinking back on my conversation with Susannah, it was clear that she had told him something about her suspicions, but she hadn't been specific about what, exactly, she had said. And there was Ellis Kirkland, the symphony's treasurer. She certainly had knowledge of Susannah's problem, but did she know that Susannah was going to talk to me? Would the police talk to her?

I decided that I could live with these risks, at least for the time being. As matters stood, regardless of what Harvey or Ellis might tell the police, the only other person who knew what Susannah had told me was dead. So as far third parties were concerned, I could probably defend my actions. I might have to do some fancy footwork, but it was my word against theirs, and I would just have to see how much I was willing to massage the facts in order to avoid prosecution.

But that wasn't an end to it. If I completed my assignment and gave a report to the symphony board, I could be putting myself back in the box. If there had been an embezzlement, and if it had something to do with Susannah's death, and if my report was revealed as a link in the chain, and if its contents were considered in relation to what I had told Hammond, and if, at that point, anybody still gave a damn, then I was condemned by my own hand. Well, that was a risk I would have to run.

My second problem was that Ellis Kirkland appeared to be the logical starting point in my investigation, if there was going to be one. How could I approach her for information on the embezzlement without blowing my cover or breaching my confidentiality obligation to Susannah? The answer to my question came to me almost right away, but now was not the time for that conversation.

I went over to my desk and wrote a condolence note to Morris Townsend.

Susannah's funeral was held three days later, in a large gothic church near her home. In the meantime, I had been to see my doctor, who ran several checks and advised that I probably had experienced a mild concussion. I was to be careful not to suffer any other head injuries. I told him I hadn't planned on suffering this one, but I would do my best.

Ed Wilson, my PR wizard, had done an expert job managing the media interest in my involvement in Susannah's murder. Even though my name had been mentioned only in passing, I had received a number of calls and e-mails expressing horror at my brush with death and gratitude for my survival. When I arrived at the church, several friends and acquaintances expressed their sympathy and concern. I thanked them and assured them that I was OK, both emotionally and physically. No one mentioned my brief incarceration.

The memorial service was heart-rending. Morrie and the kids were obviously devastated and it seemed to test the limits of their reserves simply to find their way into their pew at the front of the sanctuary. The eulogy by the senior pastor, who was a close personal friend of Susannah's, left everyone, including me, in tears. The full choir had assembled for the service, as well as a string quartet from the orchestra, and the music added to the sense of tragedy and loss. If funerals are supposed to be cathartic, the effect wasn't going to kick in anytime soon. This wasn't one of those "celebration of the life of" events; this was grief and mourning.

There was no reception or greeting of the family. The burial services were private, so at the conclusion of the service many of the attendees stood outside the church, heads down, talking in low tones among themselves and dabbing their eyes. There had been an overflow crowd. It seemed as though everyone of consequence in town was there. I saw the mayor and our congressman. Everyone I knew from the symphony board of trustees was in attendance as well as the chief executive, John Martin, and the music director with – I assumed – other members of the orchestra and staff gathered around them. Ellis Kirkland probably was part of that group, but I didn't know what she looked like. Most of the chief executives and board chairs of the city's other cultural institutions were there. Lieutenant Hammond was standing nearby, surveying the crowd. Our eyes locked for a moment, and he didn't smile. I saw Laura and walked over.

"Hi," she said, giving me a kiss. "Are you OK?" We had talked on the phone after my release and I had given her an abbreviated version of what had happened at Susannah's home and the aftermath. Laura and Susannah both had been members of a service organization when we were all young marrieds but had not stayed in close contact with each other.

"I'm fine," I assured her. "How are you?"

"It's just terrible," she said. "I can't get over it." She teared up, took a tissue out of her purse and wiped her eyes. "How could such a thing have happened?"

I had no answer to that. "I don't know," I confessed. "I just hope they find who did it." Changing the subject, I asked what she had heard from our daughter, Becky. I knew that they talked almost daily, while Becky and I usually exchanged e-mails at intervals of three or four days.

"She was shocked by Susannah's death," Laura said. "You remember that she and Nina were friends in high school." I did. Nina was Susannah's middle child.

"Are they still in touch?" I asked. "They are now," she said. "Becky said they hadn't talked much lately – Facebook friends and all that – but Becky was able to reach Nina yesterday. Nina said that she was going to drop out of college for the rest of this semester and stay home with her dad and younger brother."

"I'm sure that will be a comfort to them," I said. This disruption in Nina's life was probably just the first of many to come for the family.

"Becky is pretty upset," Laura continued. "She said Nina was blaming herself for what happened."

"How's that?" I asked.

"Well, Becky said Nina was afraid something might happen to her mother but hadn't told anyone."

5

If I was going to accomplish anything in the time I had set aside for the completion of my task, I needed to get going. The easiest place to start was with my own daughter. When I got home from the funeral, I called. She wanted to know about the service and how Nina, in particular, was holding up. I gave her my impressions, which didn't comfort her. I then moved on to what she had told her mother about Nina's state of mind. What, exactly, had Nina said?

"It was pretty disjointed," she answered. "She wasn't making much sense most of the time. She jumped from one thing to another and was crying a lot. I tried just to listen and be sympathetic and I didn't ask many questions."

"You handled it right," I said. "It was kind of you to call her. It couldn't have been an easy thing to do." I pondered whether, at her age, I would have had the guts and maturity to try to comfort a friend who had suffered such a tragedy.

"She kept saying, 'I should have listened. I should have done something.' And she also said that the whole thing might not have happened if she had told her dad what her mother told her."

"Did she say what her mother told her? Or why she didn't mention it to her dad?"

"No, and I didn't ask. As I said, I mostly just listened and sympathized. And it occurred to me that maybe Nina was over-reacting to whatever her mother had said, blowing it out of proportion because of what had happened. Nina has always had a flair for the dramatic."

"How did you leave it with her?" I asked. "Are you going to talk again?"

"I told her to call me anytime, day or night, if she wanted to talk, but I don't think I should call her again, at least not right away."

"Good girl. Listen, if Nina does call, could you let me know?"

"Sure," she said. Then, after a moment, asked the logical question. "Why?"

"Just before Susannah died," I said, "she consulted with me about a legal problem, and I agreed to help her, but she hadn't given me the details. Did Mom tell you that the police have questioned me about it?"

"Yeah," she said. "She did."

"I wasn't able to give them much to go on. As I understood it, the problem had nothing to do with Susannah, herself, but I had agreed to do what I could to sort it out and I'd like to honor that commitment if I can. I can't imagine that this problem had anything to do with her death, but if Nina tells you something that makes that connection, then I need to tell the police." I meant it. I wasn't going to withhold that information.

"So what am I looking for?" she asked. Smart girl. I hadn't raised no dummy.

"I don't know," I said, truthfully. "Susannah hadn't seemed worried about her safety when she talked to me. So I guess the question is, what did Susannah say to Nina that made her think her mother needed protection?"

"OK, Dad," she said. "I'll let you know if Nina calls."

We said good bye and hung up.

Again I considered calling Hammond. "I was talking with my daughter today, who is a friend of Susannah's daughter, and she said…." I wouldn't have to go into what Susannah had told me. On the other hand, I wasn't anxious to create new reasons for Hammond to link me to the crime, and I was pretty sure I didn't know anything that he didn't know as well. Surely the police had talked to the family members and explored all of their recent interactions with Susannah. If Nina knew what Susannah was worried about, the police probably did also. Even if Nina had been vague in her conversation with

Becky, when the investigators sat down with Nina they would have thoroughly probed her memory for all of the details of her conversation – or conversations – with her mother. I didn't call.

The next morning I telephoned Ellis Kirkland. I got her assistant; Ms Kirkland was in a conference and couldn't be disturbed. Using a vague statement about symphony business, I secured an appointment for two o'clock that afternoon. In the meantime, I logged on to the Internet and spent some time refreshing my knowledge about embezzlement. I wasn't surprised to find a wealth of information, but I was astonished at how much of it was pitched to the aspiring embezzler. Everything a potential thief would need to know, right down to sections on how to react when you looked into the mirror and saw a criminal looking back. Most of this advice boiled down to accepting the fact that you needed the money more than your boss did and lists of reasons why you might consider yourself badly treated by people who trusted you and provided you with a good job, health benefits and a living wage. After logging off, I felt as though I needed to wash my hands.

When I arrived at Ellis Kirkland's office, after being escorted through a labyrinth of hallways and desks, I surmised that, if the size and appointments of her workplace were any guide, she was pretty high up in the bank's power structure. She had a large corner office with a glass-topped desk, a long credenza behind it, a sofa, and side chairs. She wasn't there when I arrived. I took a seat in one of the chairs and looked around. My surroundings didn't tell me much about the office's occupant except that she was well-organized. Her desk was clean except for a computer and a single stack of what looked like correspondence sitting exactly in its center, its edges neatly aligned with the sides of the desk. There were none of the usual pictures of family and no diplomas or awards hanging on the walls. Very sterile.

A few minutes later, Ellis walked in. She was tall, almost as tall as I was, slender and rather attractive, if a little severe. Dark hair, worn long, dark eyes, no noticeable makeup and frameless glasses. I now remembered seeing her at Susannah's funeral. She was the sort of woman you noticed, even in a crowd.

I stood and introduced myself. She said hello, shook my hand with a firm grip, gave me a nice smile, maneuvered to the far side of her desk and sat down.

"I understand you are here about the symphony?" she said.

"Yes," I said. "Susannah Townsend gave me your name." She did not seem surprised. "I understand you were friends. I'm sorry about your loss."

"She was a wonderful person and I owe her a lot. I knew she was going to meet with you. What did she tell you?"

This wasn't going the way I had planned. My strategy had been to ask her an open-ended question about the symphony's business and hope that she would mention embezzlement. That would have preserved my deniability if questioned further by Ray Hammond. I dodged, artfully I thought.

"She said that there was some problem with the symphony's finances that she thought I might help resolve, that you were the treasurer, and that you and she had discussed the problem."

Ellis stared at me for a few moments, assessing something in her mind.

"Did she tell you it was confidential?" she asked.

"Yes, and I gave her my assurance that anything I learned would be kept so."

She thought for a few more moments. "What have you told the police?" she asked. So much for regaining control of the dialogue. Now it was my turn to think for a minute.

"Listen," I said. "Is this a private conversation?"

"I'm not sure what you are asking," she said.

"I'm asking whether I can trust you." I sat forward in my chair. "I think we both have the same interest here, to help the symphony, but if we're going to continue to dance around, we're not going to make any progress and we may not have much time. If I'm right, and if your objective is to get to the bottom of Susannah's problem and keep this confidential, then we're going to have to be candid with each other and careful what we say to anyone else, including the police. Does that make sense to you?"

She actually seemed relieved. "Perfect sense," she said. "I believe we understand each other. And yes, you can trust me." She paused, and then said, "Embezzlement."

"Yes," I confirmed, "but the police haven't heard that from me."

She thought for another minute. "I believe I understand your dilemma. Well, if it makes any difference, I was the first to use the word."

"Thank you," I said. I was beginning to like Ellis Kirkland. She was smart and perceptive. "What can you tell me?"

"Unfortunately, not much. About three weeks ago Susannah met with me here in my office. She was upset. As you probably know, the symphony has been going through some rough times, financially. In some ways, we were like General Motors. We were able to pass on increases in our costs – most of which were in wages and benefits – to our customers while times were good. Now the pressure is on both for contributions and audiences. Our business is a lot more competitive than it used to be, and we can't rely as heavily on season subscribers. The Gen Y'ers don't want to make any commitments more than four hours in advance.

"And then there is our endowment. It has never been large enough to support an operation our size, and with the drop in the markets the amounts available for distribution under our spending policy have declined and won't pick up for three or four years, even if the markets continue to recover.

"As a result, there's a lot of pressure on the board and the staff to increase revenues and cut expenses. We've been looking at our strategic options and have put everything on the table for consideration, including shortening our season and reducing the size of the orchestra. We have already implemented one reduction-in-force for the staff. Our contract with the musicians' union expires at the end of this season, so there is at least a possibility that we could restructure in some orderly way and keep our core mission intact. As you might imagine, the trustees have divided into camps and there are two major factions. One group thinks that we have no choice other than to retrench; the other would sooner die than reduce the quality or quantity of our programming and believes that we can and should increase both our annual fund contributions and our endowment.

"Well, Susannah is – was – trying to juggle all this, lead the fundraising, keep the lines of communication open, and keep everyone working for the common good, but it wasn't easy. Some of our trustees are used to giving orders and can be pretty opinionated."

I nodded. I had worked both professionally and on volunteer projects with several of them.

"We are running out of time and approaching the point at which we are going to have to make some hard decisions. So, with all this going on, after swearing me to secrecy Susannah told me that she had discovered what she thought was an embezzlement."

She paused. I could see that, from Susannah's perspective, this discovery would have narrowed the symphony's options, perhaps forcing it into an uncontrolled retrenchment and downward spiral from which it couldn't recover.

"What did she say about it?" I asked.

"Only that there appeared to be a lot of money involved," Ellis said, "and that public disclosure of the problem could be devastating to our fundraising efforts. Our conversation was mostly about how we could look into what she had learned without generating any publicity. I reminded her that our regular outside audit would begin soon and told her we would have to put our accountants on notice. She understood my point, but she didn't want me to do that right away. I also explained to her what a forensic audit was and why we might need one. We agreed that a decision on that could wait. Forensic audits are expensive and the first step would be to see what the routine audit turned up. She also said that she was going to talk to Harvey Anderson, our lawyer. She seemed to think this wasn't a garden-variety embezzlement and wanted to conduct a broader investigation." Ellis paused.

"She also remembered that, about eighteen months ago, she had backed me up in an argument with the staff over my access to the symphony's computer files. I'm a certified public accountant and I like to keep a pretty close watch on the symphony's finances. The staff wasn't keen on it, but Susannah had OK'd my request for computer access to the symphony's financial records, internal bookkeeping system and donor management software. She asked whether I was willing to work with an investigator, and I said I was. She seemed relieved.

"I didn't hear anything more for a couple of weeks. Then, about a week ago, Susannah called. She said that Harvey had agreed that an internal investigation was called for and that she was going to talk to you. She said she hadn't mentioned my name to Harvey, since she had decided not to use his firm. But she didn't say anything more about what she knew."

We were back full circle and it didn't seem that there was anything more Ellis could add to what I had been told by Susannah. I told Ellis what I knew, or surmised, about the police investigation and the possibility that Susannah was concerned about her safety. Ellis was unaware that Susannah had any such concerns and had no information as to why that might have been the case. We agreed that Ellis would send me her computer files containing the symphony's routine financial reports. I didn't expect that an embezzlement would jump out at me from a review of those records, but they would give me a better understanding of the symphony's operations. We agreed it wasn't likely the police would talk with her, as there seemed to be no way they could connect her with Susannah other than through the symphony board of trustees, and there were dozens of people who shared that relationship. In any event, she assured me, she could handle it. I believed her.

We agreed that we would talk again after I had reviewed the files she was to send me. We left her office and she walked me to the elevators. She smiled again, said good bye and gave me another hand shake. Her fingers may have lingered for a moment in my palm. She wore no rings, and perhaps the absence of pictures of hubby and the kids meant that she was unattached.

I found myself hoping so.

6

I hadn't talked with Tommy Glynn since the day of the murder, so I called him as I left Ellis' building. He was home, and I drove out to where he lived with his wife, Jane, in a small house near the college campus on the old north side. They had two grown children, both of whom lived elsewhere. Tommy was in the back yard, working in his flower garden. He invited me in and we sat in his kitchen. Jane made iced tea for us and tactfully disappeared.

I had noticed that he seemed to be limping more than the last time we had been together. He had taken a bullet in the leg in the shootout that ended his career. "How are you feeling, Tommy?" I asked.

"Pretty good, considering," he said. "I sure couldn't go running down alleys and climbing over fences any more, but I get around. Kids are OK, Jane is OK," he added. "We don't have anything to complain about."

"I appreciate you coming downtown when I was being questioned," I said.

"Happy to do it," he replied. "I try to get in there every couple of weeks anyway, and I was due for a visit. Meet any new guys, keep up my contacts, see what's going on. I hope I was helpful."

"You were," I assured him. "What can you tell me about Ray Hammond?"

"Good guy," Tommy said. "Joined the force about four years after I did. We were beat cops at the same time, but never partners. I saw him around a lot; we had beers together with some of the other guys from time to time. I didn't know him all that well, but he always impressed me as a straight shooter, serious, smart. A true professional. He made detective early and had a great record in closing his cases."

"But you didn't talk with him about Susannah's case?"

"No," Tommy said. "Because of our business relationship, I didn't think I should, at least not while you were still. . . ." He hesitated.

"A suspect?" I volunteered.

"Yeah, that's the technical term." He smiled. "It just didn't seem right applying it to you."

"Thanks." I smiled back. "Tommy, how open are your contacts willing to be with you? I mean, could you keep up to date on the investigation into Susannah Townsend's murder?"

"Well," he said, "there are limits. They're not going to give me step-by-step reports, but sure, I can follow the general thread. Am I doing this for you?"

"Yes. For a couple of reasons. One, whoever killed Susannah had some reason to take a crack at me. It may just have been part of his escape from the house, but I don't want to assume anything at this point. Maybe he meant to kill me, too. If the police investigation goes off in any direction that suggests that Susannah's killer also had a reason to go after me, I'd like to know about it. I don't want to meet that guy again if I can avoid it. He also took the trouble to plant the blood and the knife on me for reasons I can't imagine. Two, as you know, I was at her house that afternoon because Susannah had asked for my help with a legal problem. I still feel an obligation to do what I can to resolve it for her. The problem had to do with the symphony, not her personally. There probably is no connection between it and her death, but if anything comes up that ties the two together, I'd like to know about it."

Tommy thought for a moment. "In that case," he said, "don't I have to know what the legal problem is?"

I had anticipated that we would reach this point. My daughter had asked the same question. "I'm sorry, Tommy, but I have to treat what I know as confidential, for the time being. Let's just leave it at this: if the police come up with anything related to Susannah's death that sounds to you as though it might involve a legal issue for the symphony, you'll let me know? We can then talk about how to handle it, and I promise that I'll follow your advice."

Tommy was quiet for a full minute. I'm sure that obstruction of justice crossed his mind, but it was me, and not him, that was doing the obstructing. He was at least one step removed from the risk I was running. But he also had to consider the need to retain his credibility with his friends on the force. He couldn't be seen as having misled them – even by an act of omission – for my benefit, if he had any interest in continuing his relationships at police headquarters. I sipped my iced tea and waited. In the end, his appreciation for what my firm had done, and continued to do, for him, and his willingness to trust me to do the right thing, must have won out.

"OK," he said finally. "That works for me."

"There is one thing in particular that I'm interested in," I said. "When Susannah and I talked on the morning of the day she was killed, she said she was going to give me something when we met at her house that afternoon. I'm curious if the police found anything that might fit."

"Was your name on it? Anything else to go on?" Tommy asked.

I said I had no idea what we were looking for. Maybe a computer disk? A flash drive? An envelope full of papers?

"OK," Tommy said, "I'll add that to the list."

With that out of the way, I moved on to the questions that had occurred to me while nursing my wound in the holding cell the night after my arrest.

"Tommy," I asked, "do you have any ideas about who might have killed Susannah? Jealous husband? Jilted lover? Maybe her husband had found someone else and wanted her out of the way…even hired her killer? Random act of violence?"

"Yeah," he said, "I've thought a lot about that, but I don't have any ideas and, from what I learned while I was downtown, the cops didn't either. That's why you were so popular there for a couple of hours. Of course, that was several days ago and the lab work wasn't in on whatever evidence they found. They will have talked to the family by now and anyone else the victim was involved with. Most homicides – other than drug deals gone bad – are crimes of passion, which means family or friends or lovers or business associates. Someone the vic was close to. That's where I'd start looking if it was up to me. I'll drop by again tomorrow and see what's new."

We refilled our glasses and talked some more. He brought me up to date on his kids, and I reported on Becky's activities at college. Jane came in and asked if I would stay for dinner, but I didn't want to impose on such short notice. I said good bye and drove back downtown. I debated heading over to Gino's, my favorite restaurant, a small Italian place on the other side of the downtown from my condo. It attracted a crowd of regulars, mostly professionals who lived and worked downtown, and most nights I could find someone I knew to eat with if I was unaccompanied.

I also thought about giving Laura a call. After our divorce, she had taken a job with a big insurance agency in town, and she also lived in the near downtown area. She fixed us dinner at her place two or three times a month if neither of us was otherwise engaged. We still had a physical attraction to each other and sometimes I wound up spending the night in her bed. I was aware that Laura's circle of friends included some male admirers who escorted her to events that required a couple, but we didn't talk about our respective social lives and I knew better than to pry. I understood from mutual friends that she had not been seriously involved with anyone since our divorce. Kind of like me. I had developed relationships with female acquaintances that sometimes led to romantic encounters, so I couldn't object if she did the same. Laura and I were a lot alike, and still friends. Sometimes we talked about getting married again, starting over. We both had matured since we split up and had some new perspectives on life and love. Maybe we could make it work.

In the end, I went home. I warmed up some left-over beef tenderloin that I had brought home from Gino's, microwaved a potato and tossed a salad while Bruno made a nuisance of himself winding around between my legs. I fed him, poured a glass of Cabernet, sat down to eat and turned on the evening news.

The lead story was that the police had made an arrest in the murder of Susannah Townsend.

7

Albert Bullard was nineteen years old. According to the news story, he had been hired by Susannah to do yard work and odd jobs around the Townsend home three days a week. Susannah had met him as a result of volunteer work she had done at a local organization that provided job and life skills training for disadvantaged youth. Albert had been in some trouble with the law and was unable to find placement in the usual outlets that the agency relied on for employment of its graduates, and Susannah had stepped in and helped him out.

The county prosecutor, Steven Randall, was shown at a press conference that he had called to announce the arrest. Randall was a hot shot criminal defense lawyer who had switched sides and run for prosecutor in the last election claiming – ironically, many thought – that the incumbent was "soft on crime." As a result of one of the frequent swings in the mood of the electorate, rather than any short-comings in the record of his opponent, he won a narrow victory. Susannah's murder was front-page news. Randall obviously had larger political ambitions and was making the most he could out of the quick arrest of her killer. He was flanked by several police officials and I could see Ray Hammond standing in the background, looking glum.

Randall didn't provide much in the way of details, but he hinted that something had gone badly wrong in Susannah's relationship with Bullard and her murder was the result. He touted the aggressive and effective work of local law enforcement that had gotten Susannah's killer off the streets and into police custody, and suggested that the solution to the crime was the result of his leadership. He assured the public of a vigorous and effective prosecution of the case by his office and said that, in view of the brutal nature of the crime and the importance of a conviction to the community, he personally would handle the trial of the accused. The image on the screen shifted to a photo of the alleged killer, a large, muscular white man with a vacant expression on his face and hard eyes. The coverage of the press conference ended, the news anchor made some trite observation about the tragic consequences of Susannah's well-meaning efforts, and then moved on to developments in the latest political scandal.

I turned off the television and ate the remainder of my meal in silence. This outcome did seem to align with what I knew. Bullard had a personal relationship with Susannah, which fit Tommy's profile of the killer. The relationship might have involved some risk, given Bullard's background. Susannah may have become frightened of Bullard and might have mentioned some problems in their relationship to her daughter. Depending on what Nina had heard from her mother, she might have considered, and then rejected, alerting her father to the problem. Bullard would have had easy access to the house and knowledge of its layout. He certainly looked capable of a violent crime and strong enough to have killed Susannah with one knife thrust. He wouldn't have had any trouble knocking me out, and he looked dumb enough to have thought that that he could frame me for the crime.

If Bullard's arrest wrapped up the question of who killed Susannah, it also separated her murder from the problem she had left with me. Bullard certainly wasn't embezzling from the symphony. Under this scenario, I no longer had to contemplate my possible arraignment on an obstruction of justice charge and I could set aside the latent anxiety that I might be standing in the way of a solution to Susannah's murder. But on the other hand, a possible lead into an understanding of what – if anything – had happened at the symphony was now eliminated. If the embezzlement wasn't related to Susannah's death, then I had one less place to start in sorting out the facts.

Just then the telephone rang. It was Becky. Nina had called and told her about Bullard's arrest. What Becky had to report confirmed much of my hypothesis.

Nina had told the police investigators that her mother told her that Bullard had made some suggestive remarks and pawed at Susannah when they were both in the garage putting away some lawn furniture. Susannah had pushed him away and yelled at him, and told him that if he ever did anything like that again she was going to fire him on the spot and report him to the police. Her mother had been frightened but she didn't want Nina to tell her father. Her father had always been protective of her mother, Nina said, and Susannah was concerned that Morris might blow the circumstances out of proportion. She told Nina that she was going to keep Albert at arm's length and out of the house, and that he had apologized and seemed chagrined at his conduct. She didn't want to make the situation worse, and she thought that she had matters under control.

"But Nina was still blaming herself," Becky said.

"I guess that's inevitable," I said, "but she was only following her mother's directions."

"That's what her dad and everyone else have told her," Becky said. "Nobody could blame her for what happened."

"Did Nina mention any other reasons why her mother might have been upset?" I asked.

"No," Becky said. "It seemed clear to me that Nina thought it was all about Albert Bullard. She also said that was all the police seemed to be interested in."

I thanked Becky for calling, we chatted some more and hung up. I cleaned up the dishes, retreated to my study and logged on to my e-mail. Bruno followed along and jumped up on my desk, curling up on the far corner where, at least in his opinion, he wouldn't be in the way. His tail flicked back and forth across my calendar.

There were a number of messages including one from Ellis Kirkland with two attachments. The message read: "Call me after you have reviewed this." I opened the first attachment, labeled "Symphony Reports," and found operating statements and balance sheets going back over the past three years.

As expected, the operating statements showed a pattern of declining revenues in season ticket sales, but single performance and small flexible ticket packages had held up reasonably well. Special events such as the holiday spectacular had become a big part of total sales. Nonetheless, the symphony's earned revenues were shrinking at an accelerating rate and endowment support was declining. These losses were partially offset by an increase in contributions, but they weren't making up the difference. Expenses were fairly steady. I supposed that this was because most of the labor costs were locked in under the terms of the orchestra's union contract. Staff salary expense showed a dip in the most recent year, probably as a result of the reduction in force that Ellis had mentioned, but other expenses were steadily increasing. It wasn't a pretty picture. The balance sheets didn't brighten the outlook. The key ratios between the symphony's assets and liabilities were all trending in the wrong direction, the orchestra was eating into its reserves and its available resources were approaching a critical point. The other file contained the symphony's most recent annual report to its contributors and supporters. I noticed that Susannah and Morris Townsend were listed as the largest individual contributors to its annual fund.

I hadn't expected that my review of this material would provide any insights into how someone might be embezzling from the symphony, and it didn't. I was pretty certain that what Ellis had on her computer, as extensive as it was, wouldn't tell us what we needed to know. I needed whatever it was that Susannah intended to give me.

I went back to my other e-mails and responded to all that needed immediate attention. I was about to turn out the lights and go to bed when the telephone rang again. I answered.

"Alex?" a male voice inquired.

"Yes?"

"This is Morris Townsend."

8

At ten o'clock the next morning Morris Townsend was in my office, sitting in the chair his wife had occupied six days earlier. He was a large man, well-proportioned, not overweight. Imposing. Blue eyes, greying black hair. He was dressed in a dark suit, white shirt, expensive-looking tie. His face reflected the emotional strain he was under but he still emitted the power and energy that had served him so well in his occupation.

In our conversation the night before, he had said that he wanted to meet with me as soon as possible. He didn't want to talk over the telephone. I expressed my condolences. He thanked me for the note I sent. I was surprised that he remembered it; mine must have been one of hundreds. We made an appointment for this morning. We hung up and I went to bed, wondering what was on his mind other than the tragedy he and his family had suffered.

Skipping any preliminaries, Morris began. "I found this in a drawer in Susannah's desk," he said, and reached into his jacket pocket. He extracted a thin white envelope, plain except for my name written on the front. "That's her handwriting," he continued. "I don't know what's in it, but I know she was going to meet with you on the afternoon that she..." He stopped, looked down, and then recovered. "...the afternoon that she was killed."

He stood and handed the envelope across my desk. I took it. Morris sat back down. "There's something you need to know before you read whatever is in that envelope," he said. "I don't think Bullard killed Susannah." He looked hard into my eyes, trying to read my reaction to that disclosure. I'm not certain what he saw, but whatever it was, it must not have been guilt because he then said, "And I don't think you had anything to do with it either, just so we understand each other. I wouldn't be sitting here if I did."

Several questions competed for attention in my mind. I asked the one that addressed the most startling revelation. "Why do you think it wasn't Bullard?"

"That prosecutor, Randall. I have never liked that guy." Morris paused for a moment, and then the words came out in a torrent. "All he wanted was an arrest, and he wanted it done fast. Now he's grandstanding on TV. Wants to be mayor. I don't know all that much about police work, but once they heard what Nina had to say about Bullard groping Susannah, that was it. Case closed. As I understand it, the prosecutor is supposed to stay out of the investigative work, just assess what the police come up with and then decide whether he has enough to charge the suspect. But Randall was all over the place, directing traffic and making calls on where to go next. I don't think the detective in charge, Hammond, was convinced they had the right guy. He told me that Bullard denied being at the house on the day Susannah was killed. It wasn't one of his scheduled work days. But he didn't have an alibi and they found a picture of Susannah in Bullard's room. Clipped from the newspaper. His fingerprints were in our house. Their theory is that Bullard came to the house uninvited, made another pass at Susannah, she got mad, maybe slapped him, maybe started to call the police, and he lost it. Bullard had a prior arrest on an assault charge, but no conviction. Randall decided that was good enough. The next thing I know, the investigation is closed and Randall is prancing around in front of the TV cameras." Morris choked. "And my Susannah is dead and that asshole doesn't care who killed her!"

He took out a handkerchief and wiped his eyes. His emotions had gotten the better of him and he needed some time to compose himself. I sat quietly. Any lingering questions I might have had about his culpability in Susannah's death were now eliminated. He regained control after a few minutes.

"Look," Morris said, "I'm not saying that Bullard couldn't have done it. Maybe the kid did kill her. But it doesn't feel right to me. She was upset that he put a move on her, and maybe she was a little scared of him. But Susannah was smart enough about men to have known if he posed any real danger. My problem here is that Randall is putting all his eggs in the Bullard basket. In the meantime, the trail – if there is one – to Susannah's real killer is going cold. Maybe Bullard gets some bright young lawyer from the public defender's office who spots some weakness in Randall's case, or zeros in on why there wasn't a more thorough investigation. He doesn't plead his client; he goes to trial. Two years from now a jury finds Bullard not guilty, the cops have nowhere else to go, and Susannah's real killer has gotten away with it."

He paused. "And even more, I don't want Bullard convicted if he didn't do it, and I don't think he did." He looked at me. "I just need to know."

We sat there, each of us pursuing our separate thoughts. After a minute or two, he said, "Are you going to open the envelope? If you don't want to show me what's in it, you don't have to. But if it has anything to do with Susannah's death, I'd like to know."

I pulled a letter opener from my desk drawer and slid the blade under the fold. There was a single sheet of plain paper inside with computer printing on one side. I took it out. It said:

Dear Mrs. Townsend,

I'm taking a big chance writing this. I can't tell you who I am because if anyone found out it was me I would lose my job or maybe worse. I think my boss is stealing from the symphony. I can't tell you why I think this because it would give me away. I can tell you there are a lot of papers locked up in my boss's desk day and night. I think they show what is going on. I wish I could be more help but I thought you should know.

A friend

There was no date. I pondered my next move. Could I consider Morris as an ally? Did he know that Susannah suspected embezzlement? If not, and I gave him the letter, would he want to take it to the police? Under the circumstances, was that the right thing to do? I decided that he was entitled to know the facts, regardless of what the consequences might be. But I also needed to frame the issue in a way that reflected Susannah's instructions to me.

I said, "Morrie, it's possible that the police might find this letter to be of interest in Susannah's death, but it doesn't tell me anything that I didn't already know and, out of respect for Susannah's wishes in the matter, I haven't told them what she confided to me. That information is covered by the attorney-client privilege, and I may be breaching my ethical obligations by giving this to you. I need your assurance that this won't go any further without my approval."

He thought for a full minute while I sat there, the letter in my hand. "OK," he said, "I understand."

I handed him the letter and he read it. He thought some more, seemingly trying to remember something. He then said, "It's beginning to fit together. It was obvious that Susannah was worried about something related to the symphony. I tried to get her to talk to me about it, but she wouldn't. She didn't have enough facts, she said. She told me she was going to see if you could find out more. We had lunch downtown after she left your office, before she went home for your meeting there. She didn't tell me what you and she had talked about but she was relieved that you were going to help her and she thought she could trust you. I guess she was right. Thank you."

More thinking. Morris had a lot of catching up to do, and I didn't rush him. Finally, he said, "I don't want to give this to the police. Randall has his mind made up. After his big show yesterday he isn't going down any path that suggests he made a mistake in charging Bullard. We'd have to have a lot more than this" – holding up the letter – "to get his attention. Not to mention the damage that a leak would do to the symphony. But if this has anything to do with Susannah's death, I want to know what it is."

His response had opened a door and I stepped through it.

"Morrie, you could be a big help in sorting all this out. Are you willing to get involved?"

"Damn it," he said, "I *am* involved. My wife was killed, maybe over this. What do we do next?"

9

We spent the next hour and a half discussing our options. I told him about my conversations with Ellis Kirkland and Tommy, and he told me the rest of what he knew about the police investigation. It wasn't much. We agreed that I would talk again with Tommy and see if he could add anything to what we knew about Bullard's involvement. If there was solid evidence linking Bullard to the crime, then the embezzler wasn't Susannah's killer.

But if it wasn't Bullard, then maybe it was the embezzler. The only key to his or her identity seemed to lie in figuring out what he or she had done. If we had that, then we might be able to find the thief; and if we could find the thief, then we could look for a link between him or her and Susannah. My investigation into the embezzlement was morphing into a search for a killer. We agreed that we needed to talk with Ellis about how to handle the upcoming symphony audit. I picked up the phone and called her number. She answered, and we made an appointment for two o'clock that afternoon.

Our only lead was the anonymous letter. I asked Morrie what had happened to the envelope the letter came in. He didn't know; he hadn't found it with the letter. He said he would look through Susannah's desk again and see it if turned up, but he wasn't optimistic.

I read the letter again. Nothing new. It seemed to have been crafted so as to not reveal whether the "boss" was a man or a woman, but maybe that was just bad writing. The author wasn't going to produce the Great American Novel. Maybe the author was a secretary – administrative assistant, as they were now called. Or a lower-level staff person who reported to the embezzler. But we also had to consider the possibility that the letter had been deliberately dumbed down. It suggested that the writer was concerned about the consequences if his or her identity was discovered. Maybe it had been crafted so as to deflect attention from the writer if its contents came to the embezzler's attention. Maybe the writer was a peer, or even a superior. Maybe he or she had no working relationship with the "boss."

What were the sender's motives? Revenge for some other injustice, real or perceived? Or merely those of a concerned citizen who sees a crime and calls it in? Why, exactly, did the letter writer think his or her "boss" was stealing from the symphony? The only hard fact was the locked desk drawer.

We spent some time on that one. It seemed like a long shot. The first obstacle was access to the symphony offices. Not even Ellis could go walking down the aisles pulling on desk drawers…at least not while the occupants were there. What if we got in at night, or on a weekend? How would we get permission to do so? How would we know which drawers had been locked for the night and which were locked all the time? What would we do if we found one, or several? It didn't seem likely that the auditors would have access to material locked in a desk drawer, so we couldn't rely on them to produce this piece of the puzzle.

"Well," Morrie said, "Susannah was the chairperson of the search committee that hired John Martin, the symphony's chief executive officer. He owes her his job and John was one of her biggest fans. He and I have an excellent relationship. Given our support of the organization over the years, I'm betting that, if I asked, he would agree to cooperate with anything we wanted. It's at least a start."

We discussed how much we would have to tell John about our reasons for such an unusual request, and whether we could bring him into our confidence. I told Morrie that Susannah had told me that John didn't know about the letter. We pondered this dilemma but couldn't see a way around it. Maybe we didn't ask; maybe Ellis had a key to the offices. This was getting close to breaking and entering, and neither of us was comfortable with it. We agreed to talk about this with Ellis.

There was another line of inquiry that I thought we should pursue. "Did Susannah keep a diary?" I asked.

"No," he said, "just a calendar. I gave it and our telephone records to the police. They're supposed to get them back to me after they make copies. Do you want to see them?" I did.

Thinking further along these lines, Morrie then said, "And Susannah also kept pretty extensive personal files about her symphony activities. And her computer. The police didn't ask for them. I'll get them to you as well."

"Morrie," I then said, "there's something else that's been bothering me. If all Susannah had to give me was this letter, she could have done that when we met here in my office. There wouldn't have been any reason to set up the afternoon meeting at your house. During our meeting, she said she thought there was more to this than garden-variety fraud. She also told Ellis that there was a lot of money involved, and that doesn't show up in the letter. She must have had something more than the letter, either additional documents or someone else she wanted me to meet. At your luncheon, she didn't tell you anything more about what she had learned or the reason for the meeting with me?"

"No," he responded. "That was the way we operated, pretty much. She always said I had enough to worry about without being bothered with her problems, so she didn't talk with me about her work and I tried to leave my business at the office. She was smart and capable, and pretty independent. I really am going to miss…"

He started to choke up again but quickly recovered.

"I've got to go," he said. "I have a meeting with the lawyers handling Susannah's estate. I'll see you at Ellis' office at two." He got up. "And," he continued, "I'm your client now. What was your agreement with Susannah regarding your fees?"

I told him.

"OK," he said. "But forget about the cap. I don't care what it takes. I want answers."

"All right," I said. "But before you go there's one other thing I'd like you to think about. Is there any possibility that Susannah was killed by someone with a grudge against you?'

"The police asked me the same question," he responded. "I'm not the most popular guy around town. I've stepped on some toes. But I told the cops that I couldn't think of any reason why someone would kill Susannah in order to get back at me." He paused. "I don't like thinking about the possibility," he continued, "but I guess I can't rule it out."

We shook hands and he left.

I picked up the phone and called Tommy.

"I figured I'd be hearing from you this morning," he said. "I've been downtown. Your pal Ray Hammond isn't real happy."

"Let me guess why. He thinks they charged the wrong guy."

"You got it. His gut tells him that Bullard didn't do it. In his opinion, the evidence couldn't be less compelling. His fingerprints were in the house, but that's not surprising since he worked there. They found no trace of Susannah's blood on Bullard or his clothing. He would have had plenty of time to clean up before they talked to him, but almost every perp misses something. Ray isn't broadcasting his views, given the politics of the situation. And he doesn't have any other ideas about where to look. Even if he did, the official line is that the investigation is closed and he can't get any more time or money. He'd need something new to reopen it."

I was afraid that Bullard's arrest wasn't going to close the door on Susannah's murder, and it hadn't, at least in Ray Hammond's mind.

After a short silence, Tommy said. "I heard nothing downtown about any legal problem Susannah might have had, and nothing about any package with your name on it. Do you know anything more?"

"No, Tommy, I don't. I might in a few days. I'm still working on it, and I'll keep you informed. As matters stand, I have no facts that suggest that the legal problem had anything to do with her death."

"But it could have?" he pressed.

"Yes," I had to admit, "it could have."

"Alex," Tommy said, "as your friend and as an ex-cop, I'm nervous about your role in this. And mine. You've got a law enforcement background. I don't have to explain the risk you're running if you are sitting on something Hammond should know."

"I appreciate your concern, Tommy," I replied, "and I value your advice. I can only tell you that, at this point, I don't have anything that Ray or anyone else could use in Susannah's case. When and if I do, you'll be the first person to know." I wasn't entirely comfortable staking out this position, but I did it anyway.

"OK," he said, but with that tone suggests it really isn't.

10

Ellis Kirkland met Morris Townsend and me in the reception area of her offices. She teared up when she saw Morrie, gave him a long hug and told him how sorry she was about his loss. She escorted us to her office. We got settled and Ellis offered us coffee, which I took. Her assistant brought in a cup. Anticipating that Morrie would assume his accustomed role of lead participant in any meeting in which he was involved, I had asked him to let me manage our conversation with Ellis, given the delicacy of the situation, and he had agreed.

Once the preliminaries were out of the way, I told Ellis that Morrie had asked that I continue with my inquiries into Susannah's concerns about the symphony and that I intended to do so. I explained Morrie's reservations about Bullard's arrest and Steven Randall's motives; and I reported on my conversation with Tommy, Lieutenant Hammond's reservations and the unlikelihood of any further police investigation into Susannah's death. Full disclosure.

"However," I went on, "there's more to this, as you know. The police don't know that Susannah suspected there was a thief at the symphony. It could be relevant to their investigation, even if it's no longer active, so we may be running some risk in not telling them what we know. But we don't want to risk public disclosure of an embezzlement, and we're agreed that reporting a possible theft to the police presents that risk. So it's important that we all understand the consequences if it turns out that the symphony matter did have something to do with Susannah's death. In particular, we don't want to involve you in a situation that could damage your career or reputation. We could use your help, but there's…"

"I'm a big girl," Ellis interjected, "and I like to think that I know my way around. I know about obstruction of justice. I don't care. If what you're doing could lead to any new information about Susannah's death, count me in. She was a big help to me in my career and she got me on the symphony board. She was my friend. I'll do anything I can to help. I owe her that much."

I looked at Morrie and saw him nod, which I took as an indication that I should proceed. "OK," I said. "Thank you. The next logical step, as we see it, is the annual audit. I don't see that you have any alternative other than to advise your accountants of the possibility of embezzlement. You can do so without mentioning Susannah or her suspicions. As you know, you're going to have to sign a statement that affirms you have no such disclosures to make, as a part of their due diligence. So tell them now. It makes sense that they would want to keep that information in confidence during their work, so as not to tip off the embezzler, but it wouldn't hurt to confirm that. If they do find fraud, we'll have the benefit of their expertise in determining what it was and who committed it, and we can then decide whether to go to the police with that information or bring in the accountants' forensic team, or both. If they don't, then we're back to square one."

Ellis said that she would call the partner in charge of the audit, report to him that she had received an unconfirmed report of embezzlement from the symphony, and verify that the firm would handle the matter on a confidential basis.

I then took the envelope containing the anonymous letter out of my pocket and passed it to her. "Morrie found this in Susannah's desk," I said. "As you see, she put my name on it." She took the letter out and read it. "Does this suggest anything to you?" I asked when she was through. She thought for several moments, looking out the window of her office. The sky was dark in the west, and it looked as though a storm was building. Her face was lit by the afternoon sun, about to be obscured by the fast-moving clouds, and I was struck again by what an attractive woman she was. "No," she said, "it doesn't.

At least nothing beyond the obvious. But we can't go through the offices looking for locked drawers." That, at least, answered one of our questions.

"How large is the symphony staff?" I asked. She turned to her computer, clicked several times, printed out a two-page document and handed it to me. It contained a listing of the entire staff and their positions. I quickly counted the names and was surprised to find that there were over fifty, maybe half of whom had some relationship to the orchestra's financial or fundraising operations.

"Let's assume for the moment that one of these people wrote the letter. Do we have any information that would allow us to narrow the list?"

Ellis thought. "There aren't very many relationships among the staff that I would characterize as between a 'boss' and subordinate. It's a pretty collaborative place, by design. After all, it's an arts organization. Fine arts majors aren't into hierarchies. Of course," she added, "we don't know that the writer actually has a 'boss.' But let's say he or she does."

She took the list back from me and spent a minute reading the names. "I don't know all the staff, but I can identify a few entry-level people who might view themselves as being in a subordinate relationship with an immediate superior. All administrative assistants, all young and female."

"Any of them work in financial operations?" I asked.

"Two in the office of the chief financial officer and one or maybe two in the development department. Fundraising."

"Aren't you the CFO?"

"Well, yes, technically, at least from a corporate standpoint. But we have a staff person who is responsible for the heavy lifting. My role as treasurer is mostly supervisory."

"Tell us about the CFO and the development director," I asked. Ellis gave us a brief rundown. The former development director recently had moved on to a job in upstate New York with a more prestigious symphony and a bigger salary. The search was on for her replacement. The former CFO had retired at the end of the previous year. His position was now held by a new hire, who had been on board since April. He seemed to be settling into his job and was gaining the confidence of the board, but Ellis said that he couldn't be considered to be a known quantity.

We all sat quietly for a time, considering this information. I sipped my coffee, which had gone cold. Ellis said, "Even if we had access to some or all of the employees, we still would need a plausible reason for a conversation about embezzlement. How do we create that opening?"

An idea occurred to me. "Do you have a whistleblower policy?" I asked.

"Yes," Ellis said, "we do." Then, seeing where I was going, her eyes brightened and she went on. "And our audit committee has the responsibility to investigate matters within the policy, which include theft. As treasurer, I'm the chair of the committee. If we treat the letter as a report of a matter covered by the policy, I would have the authority to decide how to investigate it. I bring you in as a consultant to the committee. I'm pretty sure the policy allows me to do so."

She paused, thinking. "But," she added, "after we have talked with even one employee, the whole office is going to know that we're looking for an embezzler. And the thief isn't going to confess simply because we ask him a few questions. The author of the letter, whoever it was, took some pains to conceal his or her identity out of fear of reprisal…including possible physical harm. Unless he or she has had a change of heart, we can't expect any additional help from our tipster regardless of what it says in the whistleblower policy."

"Maybe, maybe not," I said. "We can make it clear that we are going to interview all of the employees, so we won't be singling anyone out. We wouldn't have to say that we are looking for a thief or that we have the letter. We just say that we are looking into a matter in accordance with the policy and we review, generically, the kinds of things the policy covers. We say that if the employee has any information about such matters, now is the time to tell us. We emphasize that we will take all necessary steps to protect the employee. We emphasize confidentiality. And we aren't looking for a confession, just a reaction – either fear or guilt, or even confusion – that tells us we need to probe more deeply. If the employee's response doesn't give us any reason to suspect that he or she is either the letter writer or the thief, we move on to the next. We could do six or eight of these conversations in an hour and finish in one business day, two at the most. There will be office gossip and speculation about what we're up to, but nothing newsworthy."

"I like it," Ellis said. "It's not perfect, but what other options do we have?"

At this point, Morrie, who had been sitting quietly, said, "I like it, too. But I think the first step is to talk with John Martin, and I think I should have that conversation. I'm ninety percent certain that he's not involved in any theft, and I think I can handle him in such a way that, if he is involved, I'll know it. If not, then I'm going to ask for his help. For his protection, I won't be specific about what we're looking for, but I'll tell him what you intend to do, and I'll ask him who reports to who."

He sat back, and then added, "I'm sorry to impose on your time like this, Ellis, and I want you both to know that I very much appreciate your help. I really don't have anywhere else to turn." His aspect softened, then stiffened again. "I'm not without influence, and if this goes south I want you to know that I'll do everything I can to protect you. In the meantime, it looks as though you two are going to be spending some time together. Good luck."

Ellis and I looked at each other. Her expression evolved into an enigmatic smile.

Lightning flashed and rain began to pound against the windows of her office.

11

Morrie called about eleven o'clock the next morning. He had met with John Martin and was convinced that Martin had no involvement in any theft from the symphony. As planned, Morrie had told Martin that Ellis would be interviewing the staff regarding a matter covered by the whistleblower policy, and that I would be participating as an outside consultant. He said nothing about what the matter was or why I was involved, and Martin had the good sense not to ask. Nor did he inquire what Morrie's role was in this situation. If he suspected that the matter had something to do with Susannah, he kept it to himself.

Martin offered to help in any way possible. Morrie requested, and Martin gave him, an organizational chart that showed the positions and reporting responsibilities of all of the staff members and the names of the persons holding each position. Morrie said he was sending it to Ellis and me by e-mail. If asked by the staff what was going on, Martin would say only that he was aware of the inquiry and that the staff members were to fully cooperate. We could use one of the conference rooms at the symphony offices for our interviews. The stage was set.

I called Ellis. She thought we should meet to discuss the order in which we would interview the names on the organizational chart and refine our approach to those interviews. She wanted to come in fully prepared. She asked if I was free for lunch, which I was. We agreed to meet at the Downtown Club, located on the top floor of her building, at twelve-thirty.

It was a beautiful, clear day after a night of thunderstorms, and cooler. I walked the four blocks to Ellis' bank, enjoying the weather and the exercise and thinking about our task. She was at the club when I arrived and had secured a table at the far end of the room, where we would not be overheard. The club, of which I also was a member, was a popular venue for power breakfasts and business lunches, and many deals had been cut within its walls. The view was outstanding, the service was always good and the waiters called you by name. The food wasn't all that great, but the consumption of gourmet meals wasn't the reason for being a member.

After we were seated and had ordered, Ellis reported that she had talked with each of the other members of the audit committee – there were only three – and told them that she was going to be investigating a sensitive matter that had come to her under the whistleblower policy. She told them that she had engaged me to assist her in this inquiry and that my services would be provided at no cost to the symphony. They were curious as to what Ellis knew, but she told them that, in her judgment, it would be premature to say anything more until her investigation was completed. She would then bring everyone up to speed. The other committee members accepted this.

We surveyed the organizational chart. As Ellis had noted, the symphony organization was fairly flat. John Martin and the music director both reported to the board of trustees. Generally, Martin's responsibilities were for the business side of the operation and the music director managed the musicians and the programming. Ellis and I decided that, based on the little we knew, we would focus on the business side. It didn't seem likely that the whistleblower was one of the musicians.

Reporting to Martin were the other principal officers – vice presidents for operations, finance, human relations, development and so forth, and each of them presided over a group of other staff – "coordinators" of this and "managers" of that. Only a handful had the title of "assistant." We decided to start with the assistants and move on up to the coordinators and the managers.

Our meals arrived and we ate, chatting about matters other than the symphony. I told her my story – home town (here), college and law school, the FBI, my law practice and Carrolton Associates. I told her about my family situation and how I knew Susannah. Ellis told me that she was from a small town in the northern part of the state. Her father ran the hardware store and her mother was a waitress. They were both active in their church, and Ellis' upbringing had been strict and simple. She had married the boy next door right out of high school, but a few months later her husband was killed in a farming accident. No children.

It was difficult for me to read Ellis' reaction to this tragedy, and she didn't elaborate. She seemed to be reporting a fact, nothing more. She had not remarried and had taken back her maiden name.

She had no particular job skills and no idea what to do next. Her life was turned around when one of her high school teachers took Ellis under her wing. The teacher had come from a well-to-do upbringing and had married the son of the owner of the town's only bank, whom she met at college. They had returned to his home town and he was poised to take over the management of the bank when his father retired. She persuaded Ellis to apply for admission to her alma mater, a small liberal arts college in Ohio. She did, was admitted and received a full-ride scholarship based on her test scores, high school record and need. She graduated magna cum laude, settled here, joined one of the big accounting firms and practiced public accounting for five years, eventually earning her CPA designation. One of the engagements to which her firm assigned her was the audit team that served the bank where she now worked. After two years on this assignment, the bank recruited her to join its staff. She had steadily moved up in the management ranks and was now the bank's chief compliance officer.

She had met Susannah through the symphony, but in the role of a consumer. By chance, they had adjacent seats at a concert and fell into a conversation. They seemed to form an immediate bond and became friends. Susannah had recently joined the symphony's board of trustees and encouraged Ellis to join one of the committees, working on audience development. Ellis liked the committee work and through it met a number of the other trustees. When, a few years later, Susannah asked Ellis if she would be interested in joining the board, she readily accepted. She confessed to Susannah that her financial situation at the time did not allow her to make the large contributions that seemed to be the price of admission to the board, but Susannah replied that all that mattered was that the symphony continued to be one of Ellis' top philanthropic priorities.

I suspected that, with the growth in her job responsibilities since then, Ellis' income and her capacity for charitable giving had significantly increased. It seemed likely that Susannah had seen a winner and taken the long view.

After our plates were cleared by the always-helpful waiters, we turned to the conduct of the staff interviews. Ellis said that she had accumulated some vacation time and was going to block out the coming two weeks. I said that our task shouldn't take that long, and she agreed; but the FDIC had recommended that all bank employees be away from their responsibilities for at least two weeks each year, and her bank had adopted that requirement. It was a fraud deterrent, she said. So if she was going to be gone at all, it might as well be for two weeks. We agreed to begin on Monday, three days hence. Ellis said she would contact John Martin and ask him to schedule our interviews.

As the concept was my idea, Ellis said, I should take the lead in the questioning. She would begin by explaining the provisions of the whistleblower policy and then turn it over to me. We would both take notes but would not record the interviews. We thought that doing so might make the subjects more nervous than they already were. We would schedule a few minutes for us to confer after each session. If either of us picked up any vibrations, we would flag that name. When we were finished with the entire process, we would then decide on how to follow-up.

It seemed simple enough at the time.

12

On Saturday morning I played golf at the country club. I had played since high school and at one time had a three handicap, but I hadn't kept up my game in recent years. This was one of those days on which I couldn't do anything right, but I had finally matured to the point where I could enjoy the exercise and the company and not let my performance spoil the outing. My foursome gathered for lunch in the club's grill room after our round. We had seated ourselves and placed our orders when I saw Harvey Anderson sitting at another table. He spotted me and walked across the room.

"Alex!" he said, with what seemed to be excessive enthusiasm. "Great to see you. Listen, could we talk for a minute?"

"Sure, Harvey," I said, excused myself and got up from the table. We walked into an adjoining lounge. No one else was there. The room was decorated in a style designed to evoke something Olde English – paneled walls, false beams, shelves stacked with books that probably had been bought by the yard, heavy mahogany furniture, dark leather upholstery and a gas fire burning in the fireplace even though it was only September. We didn't sit down.

"What's on your mind, Harvey?" I asked.

"Terrible thing about Susannah," he said. "You know, I was with her just a few days before she died."

"Oh?" I replied, noncommittally.

"Yes," he said. "Symphony business. I suggested that she might consult with you about her problem, and I was curious whether or not she had done so."

I pondered how to respond to this. On the one hand, Harvey had a perfectly legitimate interest in following up on the advice he had given Susannah. But on the other hand, whether she had or had not met with me, and what we had discussed, was between me and Susannah. I remembered that she hadn't disclosed to me what, exactly, she had told Harvey. I decided to play it down the middle, a tactic that had eluded me during my round that morning.

"We met," I said, "but I'm afraid I can't disclose what we talked about."

"Of course!" he said. "Lawyer-client and all that. But she was my client too."

"Actually, Harvey," I said, "your client is the symphony, not Susannah." He glared at me.

"Cut the bullshit, Alex," he shot back. "If she met with you, then it was to talk about symphony business; specifically" – he lowered his voice – "embezzlement. That was why I sent her to you. So that much is a given." By now he was almost hissing. "What I want to know is what she told you and what you're doing about it. As you point out, it's my client, the symphony, whose interests are at stake here. I need to know what you're up to."

"Harvey," I responded, "I'm not going to tell you 'what I'm up to' but I will confirm that I'm responding to Susannah's request, that I have discrete and confidential board-level support, and that I think I have a reasonable chance of sorting this out without it becoming public. As I understood it from Susannah, she told you to stand down and you know how sensitive this is. But if you believe you have an obligation to pursue the matter, then go to the board of trustees, tell them what Susannah told you – in confidence, as I understand it – and see what, if anything, they want you to do about it. But any damage done to the symphony as a result of that disclosure will be your responsibility."

In taking this approach I knew there was some risk that Harvey would call my bluff and do just that, in which case the matter would be out of my hands and, probably, into the headlines. But I didn't see any other way to persuade him to butt out.

Harvey stared at me. Another club member, whom Harvey and I both knew, stepped into the room, looked around, didn't find who he was looking for, waved, and walked out. It occurred to me that there might be a way to placate Harvey while at the same time giving me an exit from the situation that could keep me insulated from the attention of Lieutenant Hammond.

"Look, Harvey," I said. "I understand your interest in this. Can we leave it this way? When I've completed my inquiry, I'll let you know what, if anything, I have found. I should be done with this in a week or two. If there is anything that should go to the board, you can step in and run that process and I'll back out. There's no reason for me to stay involved beyond that point."

I was pretty sure this would be OK with Morrie and Ellis, under the circumstances.

Harvey thought it over. "OK," he said. "I can give you a couple of weeks, if that's the way you want it. But don't screw this up." And he walked back into the grill. I followed, not overly distressed about his lack of confidence in my abilities.

I sat back down at my table. A cold beer was waiting for me. I took a swallow. Very refreshing.

"What did Harvey want?' asked Ted Crawford. The other two guys at the table were engrossed in a conversation about the prospects of the football teams at the various colleges around the state. Ted also was a lawyer. He had started out in practice with my old firm at about the same time I did but left after four or five years to go in-house with one of the big insurance companies headquartered in the city. He was now the company's general counsel.

"I think he just wanted to deprecate my legal skills," I said. Ted laughed.

"That would be Harvey. He never lets a chance go by. Did you notice who he's sitting with over there?"

I looked over. I was stunned to realize that the man with his back to us was Lieutenant Ray Hammond. "I only know one of them," I said.

"I'm pretty sure that none of them are members," Ted said. "The guy to Harvey's right is Jason Plaskett. He's Steve Randall's chief deputy. What could they be talking about?"

I stole another glance in Harvey's direction. Plaskett was a beefy young man with a buzz cut who looked as though he might have played college football. He was dressed in a business suit, rather uncomfortably it seemed, even though it was a Saturday.

The only thing I could think of that connected Hammond – and Plaskett – to Harvey was Susannah. Had Hammond made that same connection and was he probing Harvey for other leads? Was Harvey, at this moment, telling him that Susannah's meeting with me was about embezzlement? But why would he do that, after our just-concluded pleasantries in the club lounge? I was pretty sure that we had reached an understanding – unless he had just been stringing me along after deciding to throw me to the wolves. And wasn't the investigation closed? And if it wasn't, why was it being conducted in the grill room of the country club? That didn't seem likely. Whatever it was, the participants had no qualms about being seen together in a public place.

Ted was one of those guys who liked to know about people: who knew who and how. He wasn't a gossip, just someone who enjoyed understanding connections, and he seemed to have a bead on almost everyone in town. Ted was a walking encyclopedia when it came to the trees of the city's old families. I decided it might be productive to reveal Hammond's identity.

"The guy with his back to us is a cop. He was the chief investigator in Susannah Townsend's murder," I said. "He interviewed me. His name is Ray Hammond."

"Huh!" said Ted. He thought a few moments. "I've heard that Randall is interested in running for mayor. Maybe it's about politics."

"I don't think Harvey would let himself be pulled into partisan politics," I responded. "He's too cautious. He might wind up having backed the wrong horse and find himself on the outside of the next big deal."

“Maybe he’s working both sides of the street,” Ted suggested.

“In the grill room of the country club? And a police officer wouldn’t be a party to any political intrigues.”

“You’re right,” he responded. “That can’t be it.”

“Do you know who the fourth guy is?” I asked.

Ted looked over to Harvey’s table again.

“Yeah,” he said. “That’s Chris Goodman. He’s a partner of Harvey’s. Specializes in criminal law.”

Involuntarily, my head spun back in Harvey’s direction. He looked up, saw me staring at him, and smiled.

13

At eight-thirty on Monday morning I met Ellis in the reception area of the symphony's offices. John Martin came out to greet us. Ellis introduced me. He was trim, average height, animated and professional. Martin said that he had everything set up for our interviews, and led us to a conference room adjacent to the reception area. I could see staff cubicles and offices farther down the hallway. Befitting a non-profit operation, the accommodations seemed adequate but not luxurious. Martin had arranged for coffee and rolls and told us to make ourselves at home. He gave us a schedule of our interviews. He said that, with time for lunch and breaks, it was going to take two days to get through the entire list, and he hoped that was all right with us. It was. The staff was curious about what was going on, he said, but no one had refused to participate. He asked us no questions about our mission, and left.

At eight-forty five, our first interviewee knocked timidly on the door and Ellis opened it. A small, rather mousey young woman came in. She looked as though she was just out of college.

"Hi," she said. "I'm Susie Warren?" She said her name as though it were a question.

"Hi, Susie," Ellis said. "I'm Ellis Kirkland. I don't think we've met. This is Alex Carrolton. He's helping me with these interviews."

"Hi." Susie said again. I smiled and said hello. Susie sat down at the table. Ellis came around and sat next to me, opposite Susie. I opened my file. Susie was the administrative assistant to the development director.

Ellis said, "Susie, as you know from John, I'm here in my capacity as chair of the audit committee. Alex and I are looking into a report of conduct that could indicate wrongdoing involving the symphony. We appreciate your talking to us. How long have you been with the symphony?"

"Only three months," Susie answered. "I graduated from college in June."

"Was our whistleblower policy explained to you when you were hired?"

"Yes. I have a copy. I read it again yesterday."

"Then you understand that, under that policy, anything you tell us will be held in confidence. We're going to talk with all of the staff, so no one will be able to identify the source of any information we might be given. The only way in which you might be connected with the matter is if it turns out to involve a crime and we have to bring in law enforcement. Also, under the policy, no one will be allowed to retaliate against you because of anything you might reveal to us."

"Yes," Susie said, in her soft voice, "I understand."

"And you understand the kinds of matters that the policy covers?" Ellis asked.

"Yes, I think so. Theft, improper financial transactions, that sort of thing."

"That's right, and you also should think about situations within the office that might create an atmosphere in which that sort of thing could happen. Romantic involvements, for instance."

"OK," Susie said. So far, she had been calm and seemingly unconcerned about the circumstance in which she found herself. Ellis looked at me, seemed satisfied that she had carried out her part of the interview, and indicated that I should take over.

"Susie," I began, "Tell us about your job here. What exactly do you do?"

"Well," she said, "I work in the development department. I guess you'd say I'm the low person on the totem pole, so I do pretty much whatever needs to be done. Answer the phones, run copies, open the mail, prepare letters, help the other staff prepare for special fundraising events, that sort of thing. But mostly I schedule meetings for the development director and help her prepare for them. Of course, she's gone now and her replacement hasn't been hired, so we're not doing much of that at the moment."

"What kind of meetings?" I asked.

"Oh," she said. "Well, mostly meetings with people who give us money. Our big contributors. Some are individuals, some work for our sponsors, some for foundations, people like that."

"What do you do to prepare for those meetings?"

"I check our computer files, look up what people have given us in the past, review any letters they might have sent us or notes of conversations they might have had with people on the staff, look for any changes in their families or businesses that might be important. We subscribe to a database that tracks a lot of stuff that can be important in deciding what to ask a person to give, and I review that. If it's a foundation, I check its website to see if there have been any changes in its grant requirements, and I look at its most recent Form 990. Then I prepare a summary."

"Can anyone on the staff get access to the data you're describing?" I asked.

"Well, the stuff on the Internet anyone can see, of course. But as for the personal data, no. It's very confidential. Some people are very protective of their privacy and even more so about their personal financial information. You might be surprised how much we know. Only the people in the development department can see it, and we're sworn to secrecy."

"So these records are kept under lock and key?" I asked.

"Well," said Susie, "Most of it is in the computer, and we're the only ones with the passwords. But, sure, any paper documents are kept locked up when they're not being used."

I didn't stop to calculate the odds of hooking our letter-writer on the first cast, but I saw no reason not to ask a leading question. "In the director's desk?" I suggested. I watched closely for her reaction, but there wasn't one. In the same even tone she said, "Yes, sometimes, but each of us in the department has a lockable file drawer in our work area. We all have confidential documents from time to time."

I switched gears and wrapped up. "Let's go back to Ellis' explanation of why we are here. We have reason to believe that something may have happened that would be covered by the whistleblower policy. If you have any knowledge, or suspicions, you can – and should – tell us what you know. Anything you say will be handled in the manner described in the policy. This is important to the organization. Is there anything you can tell us?"

Susie looked both worried and helpful at the same time. "Gee," she said, "I wish I could help, and I would, but I really don't know anything."

Both Ellis and I thanked her for her time, and she left the room. The interview had taken less than ten minutes. The thought crossed my mind that this was going to be a waste of time unless we got very lucky.

Sure enough, by noon we had talked to a dozen people and hadn't learned anything. Each of the interviews had gone pretty much the same way and they were beginning to run together in my mind. Everyone seemed anxious to help; no one knew anything. I had learned more than I wanted to know about the back office operations of a symphony orchestra.

Ellis and I broke for lunch and walked to an up-scale deli located on the ground floor of one of the nearby office buildings. We went through the line, got our food and found a table.

"I didn't think this would be boring," Ellis said, "but it is. Are we asking the right questions?"

I thought about that. "I don't see that we can be any more specific about what we are looking for without risking a leak. It is tedious work, but we knew it would be. This is, after all, a long shot."

Ellis pushed her salad around on her plate. "I know," she said, "and I'm not complaining. But I am thinking you owe me a nice dinner when we get through with this. It was your idea." She smiled.

"You're on," I said.

14

The afternoon session went pretty much as the morning. We were working our way up the organizational chart and talking with staffers who had a greater breadth of knowledge about the organization and broader responsibilities, but we weren't learning anything that would lead us to a suspected embezzler. We finished the day having met with about half the staff.

Ellis had a meeting that evening of one of the other organizations she volunteered for. I went back to my office and caught up on some matters that needed attention, and then went home. Bruno was glad to see me, at least to the extent that a cat is ever glad to see anyone. I fixed and ate my dinner, settled into my recliner with a Civil War history that I had been reading, turned on the Monday night football game for background noise and promptly fell asleep.

Ellis and I were back in our conference room at eight forty-five the next morning, ready for our first interview of the day. It and the rest of the morning interviews were uneventful. Then, after lunch, we came to Josie Jackson, the personnel manager. Josie was a no-nonsense type. A large, imposing woman. Ellis went through her routine about the purpose and terms of the whistleblower policy, but before I could get started with my questions, Josie had one of her own.

"Does this seem like one big happy family to you?" Ellis and I both stared at her. "Well, it's not. We're no different from most businesses. We have our little office intrigues. Do you know why Ann Conway left?" I looked at Ellis.

"Our former chief development officer," she explained to me. "No," she said to Josie. "I understood that she got a better offer in New York."

"Well, she did," Josie replied, "but that's not why she left. She was having an affair with someone at the symphony – I don't know who – and it turned ugly. I think the guy was married. For some reason – I don't know why – she came out on the short end. John didn't ask my advice on how to handle it. He told her that she was going to have to leave and that, if she was willing to go quietly and not make a fuss, he could get her a great job. Apparently she took him up on it. Big going-away party, everyone smiling and saying how much we would miss her, wishing her good luck. And she left. We probably dodged a bullet, from a legal standpoint. Nobody knew the real reason she was going."

"How did you find out?" I asked.

"John told me, after the fact," she said. "I had to OK the terms of her severance. They weren't out of line or anything – the same deal we would have given anyone in Ann's position. The quid pro quo was the new job. Harvey Anderson's firm signed off on the terms and drafted her severance agreement. It had some additional boilerplate in it about confidentiality and each of us waiving our rights against the other, and John felt that I should understand the background. The agreement went into her file in my office."

"There was no suggestion that Ann was involved in any financial improprieties?" I asked.

"That's why I mentioned it," Josie said. "I'm not aware of anything along that line, but Ann lived a good life here – nice car, expensive clothes, nice apartment, nice jewelry. Nothing ostentatious really, but her lifestyle seemed out of line with her income, at least what we were paying her. Maybe she had an inheritance or something. I know she had been married before; maybe she got a nice settlement from her ex. Maybe she was getting presents from her boyfriend. In any event, she liked having money and nice stuff and she seemed a little obsessed about it. I think that's the reason she took the deal John offered her –

more money. Me, I would have told him where to stick it. But I can't point to anything specific."

"And you don't know who she was having the affair with," I inquired.

"Nope," she responded. "I'm not even sure John knows, and I don't know how the problems with her boyfriend came to his attention." Josie stood up. "That's all I got. Nice talking with you." And she walked out.

Ellis seemed stunned. "I had no idea," she said. "I guess I can see why John handled this the way he did, and it doesn't seem as though he did anything improper, but still…"

"I agree," I said. "Under the circumstances, it doesn't seem like the sort of thing a CEO would do without some authority from his board. I wonder if he talked with Susannah about it."

"We need to ask him," Ellis said.

The remainder of our interviews turned up nothing of interest. We finished the day by talking to John Martin. We met in his office. One wall was lined with shelves jammed floor to ceiling with books about music, performers and orchestras. There were a lot of plaques and awards on the other walls. The furniture looked as though it had been salvaged from some liquidation sale. Nothing fancy. We talked generally about the operations of the symphony and his responsibilities. He was intelligent and articulate, as I expected he would be. He didn't pry into what we had learned over the past two days.

After the preliminaries, Ellis launched into her routine. She said she was sure he was familiar with the terms of the whistleblower policy; he said he was, and went on to say that he was anxious to help us in any way he could. My turn. The only thing I wanted to ask him about was Ann Conway, but a direct question would reveal the source of our information about her. Also, I wanted to see how forthcoming he would be, so I approached the subject obliquely.

"First, let me say that we don't know exactly what we are looking for. We have information that suggests that an improper financial transaction described in your whistleblower policy may have occurred, but we don't know what. The situations covered by whistleblower policies can arise out of just plain greed and opportunity, but more frequently they're the result of a financial problem encountered by a member of the staff – unanticipated medical expenses, a spouse's loss of his or her job, and so on – or because of some personal relationship among staff members that gives one of them access to high-level information and a special opportunity." John was attentive but impassive. He undoubtedly had heard much the same information from Morris Townsend.

"I've read your auditor's reports and their comment letters for the past few years," I continued, "and the symphony's procedures for handling its accounts seem to be state of the art, so it doesn't seem likely that you would be the victim of common theft by an insider. No real 'opportunity.' That leaves the more esoteric stuff, and I guess we can't rule out theft in response to some financial hardship. Does anything of this sort come to mind? I think we can narrow the time frame to the last twelve months."

John thought for several moments. He seemed to have some difficulty deciding what to say next. Finally, he began.

"I…well, this is awkward." He paused, then continued. "This past summer we did have a…situation…with a staff member, but it had nothing to do with the symphony's finances. We had to let someone go for reasons related to personal conduct."

"Who was that?" I asked.

"Our development director, Ann Conway."

"What was the problem?"

Martin now seemed ill at ease. "I'm not sure how much I can tell you. We have a confidentiality agreement with Ann, and there are other…considerations."

I thought for a few moments, reflecting back on our conversation with Josie Jackson.

"Can you tell me how you became aware of the problem?" I asked.

Martin looked at me, and then at Ellis, and then said, "I have a question for you. Why is Morris Townsend involved in this?"

Seeing that a full explanation would lead us where we didn't want to go, Ellis attempted to gloss over the facts. "Morris came into possession of some information related to the symphony that he passed on to me after Susannah's death," she said. "I told him I would look into it, and that's why we're here."

"Did the information come from Susannah?" Martin asked.

"Is that important?" I asked. I was getting a little peeved, and it may have shown in my voice. Martin recoiled slightly.

"I'm sorry," he said, "I'm not at liberty to answer your question."

"Your source was Susannah, wasn't it?" I asserted. "She told you something about Ann Conway that led to her departure."

Martin said nothing.

"I assume," I continued, "that Susannah instructed you to keep what she told you confidential, and to not identify her as the source of the information, and that's why you won't tell us. Is that right?"

"I want to talk to Morris," Martin responded, "before I say anything more."

"OK," I said. "Call him. We'll wait. We'll be in the conference room." I stood up, and Ellis followed me out of the office.

15

Ten minutes later Ellis and I were on our way out of the symphony offices. Martin had returned to the conference room and told us that he had been unable to reach Morris Townsend. He was apologetic but refused to continue with us until he had done so. He promised to call me. We said good bye, thanked him for his help with our interviews and left. It was warm but the sun was sinking below the tops of the downtown buildings. I took out my phone and called Morris. No answer at his home or on his cell phone. I left messages at both numbers asking that he call me before he talked with John Martin. I then called his office and, even though it was after business hours, someone answered. I was advised that Mr. Townsend was out of the city until tomorrow. I left a message for him to call me.

"I think we've done all we can for today," I said to Ellis. "Are you available tonight for our dinner date?"

"Why, yes," she answered. "That would be lovely. Are drinks included? I could use one."

"Indeed they are. Why don't I pick you up at your place about eight?"

"Perfect," she said, and gave me her address. We parted and headed for our cars. I went home, fed Bruno and showered, thinking about where we might go for dinner. Ellis lived in a subdivision on the northeast side of town. There was an excellent seafood restaurant not too far from her house. I called and made a reservation. I put on slacks and a blazer and headed for Ellis' place.

When Ellis answered the door, for a moment I wasn't sure I had the right address. She had somehow changed her hair, the rimless glasses were gone and she was wearing a very becoming outfit that showed off her willowy figure to great advantage. "Wow!" I said, involuntarily.

"Why, thank you," she said, and smiled. She picked up her purse and a light wrap and I let her into the passenger seat. Ten minutes later we were at the restaurant. We were seated in a booth along the far wall. I noticed that the eyes of several of the male patrons – and one or two of the women – followed Ellis as we were led across the room to our table. We ordered drinks, martinis, hers straight up with an olive and mine on the rocks with a twist.

"Well," I said when they arrived, "here's to crime."

"Without which we might not have met," she added, and we touched glasses and sipped. "That," I said, "hits the spot." We studied the menus and chatted about entrees we had ordered on previous visits to the restaurant. Ellis seemed to favor the more exotic dishes; I admitted that my tastes were pretty straightforward. The waitress came and took our orders – salads, entrees, side dishes, how we wanted the fish prepared. She wrote nothing down; I don't know how they do that. I ordered a bottle of Pinot Gris, to be served with dinner.

Our conversation turned to our meeting with John Martin. "I'm having some trouble putting all this together," Ellis said. "Susannah seems to have been the source of John's information about Ann Conway, do you agree?" I did, as that view also solved the question of who authorized Martin to fire her. "But how did Susannah get that information? I think it's strange that she never said anything to me about it. And why did she decide – if she did – that Ann had to leave? Was there more to it than the affair? Was Ann stealing from the symphony? If so, why would Susannah just let her walk out the door? And the timing doesn't suggest any connection with the embezzlement. Ann left in early August. Susannah's first conversation with me about the embezzlement was several weeks later. And I can't imagine John pulling strings to get Ann a new job if he knew she was embezzling. Maybe Susannah just told him she had to go and didn't say why, but I guess my initial conclusion is that Ann's departure and the embezzlement aren't related."

"Maybe not," I agreed, "but let's not rule anything out. There wasn't any date on the whistleblower's letter, remember, and we don't know how long Susannah had it before she talked to John. All we really know is that, by that time, the matter had become urgent in her mind. And since she seems to have had no hard evidence that Ann was stealing, she might have been satisfied just to see her gone."

We both thought for a few moments. "How well did you know Conway?" I asked.

"We talked on a number of occasions," Ellis replied, "but we weren't close. She usually sat in on the meetings of one of my board committees. There was something about her that I found a little off-putting. Maybe Josie Jackson is right; that Ann's primary interest is Ann."

"What the situation suggests to me," I said, "is that we need to talk to her. See if we can uncover some connection between her resignation and the embezzlement, or rule it out entirely. That's the only real lead we have after two days of effort."

"That's going to be a difficult conversation. We're not supposed to know why she left the symphony, so we can't ask about the affair. If she's a thief, she certainly isn't going to volunteer that information. She'll just say she got a better offer and took it."

"It won't violate any confidence for us to ask why she left," I said. "If she lies about it, that tells us something – although maybe not much, since John has provided her with a cover story and Ann isn't under any legal obligation to tell us the truth. And we can ask her how she supported her lifestyle here on the salary she was getting from the symphony. In any event, if Morrie is willing to pay the airfare, I think we should fly out and see her. We don't know what she'll say until we ask. We take the dawn patrol out, have our meeting, and we can be home that night."

Ellis thought about it. "OK," she said, "I agree."

We talked some more. Our dinners and the wine arrived and we ate. The food was excellent and the wine was satisfactory. We lingered over coffee and split a dessert. It was about ten-thirty when we left, and the place was almost empty. Ellis put her arm through mine as we walked to the car.

"I've enjoyed the last two days," she said, "being with you."

"Me too," I replied. I meant it. I liked her…a lot. But I was having some trouble sorting out what I was feeling. I found her attractive, no question, and I had no difficulty conjuring up images of us in bed together, our clothes off, locked in some erotic embrace. The possibility – exhibit A being her arm entwined in mine – that she might share this vision didn't make it any easier to unscramble my thoughts. Then, suddenly, I found myself thinking about Laura.

As if reading my mind, Ellis withdrew her arm. We reached the car and got in. There was an awkward silence between us as we drove to her house. I found it odd that my ex-wife would come to mind just as I was contemplating the consummation of a new relationship. If I was having second thoughts about our divorce, why now? I had enjoyed physical relationships with other women without flashbacks to my married life. Then it dawned on me: there was a qualitative difference about my feelings for Ellis. It wasn't that I wanted Laura back; it was that I was prepared to give her up…for good. No more sleep-overs; no more speculation about our possible re-marriage. But it didn't feel right, jumping into a serious relationship with someone else, before I told Laura how I felt. She was, after all, the mother of our daughter and we clearly had some sort of continuing relationship.

On the other side of the equation was Ellis. I had known her for less than a week, and we hadn't even held hands, but I didn't want to mess this up. All of a sudden, my urge to get in bed with her was trumped by the fear that it could turn out to be a one-night stand. Maybe we would both have second thoughts in the morning, or maybe a sexual encounter at this stage would complicate things for her – and us – later on.

We arrived at Ellis' house. She was tense. I stopped the car, screwed up my courage and asked, "Could I come in for a few minutes? I won't ask to stay, but I want to talk. About us."

16

I didn't leave Ellis' house until eleven-forty five. I turned on my phone when I got in the car, and the message indicator beeped. It was from Morris Townsend. He was home, had received my message and would be up until at least midnight. I called back, and he answered on the first ring. I reported on our interviews with the symphony staff, why John Martin had called him, and our conclusion that the next step would be to talk with Ann Conway. Morrie said that the Conway story was news to him. He couldn't confirm that Susannah was the source of Martin's information, but he wouldn't be surprised if she was. She kept a close watch on everything going on at the symphony and her grapevine kept her supplied with information from several sources. He thought Conway was a tramp and hadn't been sorry to see her go, and he said that Susannah shared his views. He OK'd the plane fare.

We talked about how to handle Morrie's response to Martin. There didn't seem to be any good reason to connect Morrie to our investigation more closely than he already was. We agreed that it did no harm for us to assume that Susannah was the source of Martin's information about Conway and that – for the time being, at least – we didn't need Martin's confirmation of that fact. If the interview with Conway turned up nothing, we could always go back to Martin and increase the pressure for information about what he knew. We agreed that Morrie would tell Martin that he should use his own judgment about what to say to Ellis and me. We said goodnight and hung up.

I started the car and drove away. I was euphoric about my conversation with Ellis. She had made coffee and we sat in her living room. I couldn't tell what she was thinking, but I sensed that she was ready to listen and hopeful that I would say something to release the tension between us. I didn't pull any punches. I didn't see any reason to. I told her that I found her very attractive, that I had become very fond of her in the short time we had known each other and that I was hopeful our relationship would grow. I said that I was not presuming that she had any serious interest in me, but I hoped she did. If not, then I asked that she accept my apology for putting her in an awkward situation and said that I wouldn't let my feelings – or hers – interfere with our continued business relationship. Finally, I told her that, until just now, I hadn't realized that I was confused about the situation with my ex-wife. I was now certain that it would not be an obstacle to our future relationship, if there was to be one, I said, but I wanted to sort things out with her first.

Ellis stood up, crossed over to the sofa, sat down next to me and gave me a kiss on the cheek. She took my hands in hers and said that she felt as I did and had the same hopes for us. She thanked me for telling her how I felt. She said that she, too, had some baggage left over from her marriage and its tragic outcome and that she didn't want to rush things, but she also wanted our relationship to grow. She would tell me more later, but now was not the time.

We sat there, holding hands for a couple of minutes. It felt right. We seemed to have reached some sort of understanding. I said I should be going. We stood, and then fell into a full embrace, our arms around each other, and kissed. I ran my hand down her spine and pressed her more tightly against me. She yielded easily. The kiss grew longer and more passionate. For a minute I thought we were going to lose our resolve and fall back onto the sofa, but we recovered and disentangled, grinning like a couple of teenagers. She walked me to the door, we kissed again and said goodnight.

At my office the next morning I returned phone calls and e-mails. I called Ellis and told her that Morris had agreed to cover the expense of a visit with Ann Conway. We agreed that she would call Ann, and

I gave her the dates on which I had conflicts for this week and the next. Her cover story would follow the same approach we used with the current symphony staff: that we were pursuing a matter covered by the whistleblower policy and wanted to talk with her about it.

My assistant came in with checks that needed signing. I felt as though I should bring Tommy up to date, although there wasn't much I could tell him. I called and we agreed to meet for lunch. One of my partners wanted to talk about some tax issues that had come up in a problem he was handling, and I spent an hour with him. I worked on a brief that was due later in the month in one of my pending court cases. I had told the client that the case was a loser, but he wouldn't give up and could afford to pay the bills. It was a matter of principle, he said. Funny how that and having a large sum of money at stake often went together.

Shortly before noon the phone rang. It was Ellis reporting that she had reached Ann. The conversation hadn't gone well. Ann wanted to know more. She was guarded and defensive. She didn't see any reason to talk with us; she wasn't at the symphony any longer and all of that was behind her. She had moved on, she said. Ellis hadn't taken no for an answer. She told Ann that this was important and that she owed it to the symphony to help us if she could. We would only take up an hour or so of her time. After a lot of foot-dragging, Conway finally agreed and they set a date for a meeting on Friday, three days hence. I said that I would get us plane tickets. I gave that assignment to my assistant and left the office.

On the way to my luncheon with Tommy I remembered that I had promised Lieutenant Hammond that I wouldn't leave town without telling him. I called his number and he answered. I said that I had an out-of-town business engagement on Friday but that I would be back that evening. He thanked me for calling.

I met Tommy at a sandwich shop in a small commercial area near his house. We ordered, got our food and took a table. After the usual pleasantries, I asked if he had heard anything more about Susannah's case.

"Steve Randall has brought in Jason Plaskett to prepare the case against Bullard," he said. "Plaskett's his chief deputy. Not the sharpest knife in the drawer, unfortunately, but very loyal to Randall. Told Plaskett to dig a deep hole in which to dump Bullard. This is one case Randall doesn't want to lose."

"I saw Plaskett at the club on Saturday," I said. "He and Ray Hammond were having lunch with two other guys, both lawyers – Harvey Anderson and Chris Goodman. Do you know them?"

"Goodman, the criminal defense lawyer? Yeah, I've heard of him. I don't know Anderson."

"Any idea what that would have been about?"

Tommy thought, taking a bite from his sandwich. "It wouldn't be unusual for the prosecutor's office to bring in an outside expert to help prepare for a major trial," he said. "Test what arguments they might anticipate from the defense, look for holes in their own case. There's money in the office budget to pay for it, or at least there used to be. But the country club seems like an odd place for a semi-official meeting." He took another bite. "Let me see if I can find out anything from Hammond."

"Thanks," I said.

"There's one other thing you might want to know."

"What's that?"

"Ray Hammond isn't a fan of Randall's. Back when Randall was still in the criminal defense business, Ray arrested a guy on a felony murder charge. The perp was the driver for a guy holding up a liquor store. The clerk hit the alarm and pulled out a sawed-off from under the counter. He fired and winged the robber, but the robber fired back and the clerk was killed. Ray was in a black and white only a couple of blocks away and arrived at the scene as the bad guys were pulling out. He cut off the getaway car and rolled out the driver's side door, weapon drawn. The shooter ran, but the driver got off three rounds at Ray before Ray took him down. Shot him in the gut. The slug went through him and did some spinal cord damage but, surprisingly, the guy lived. He hires Randall as his lawyer, and at the trial he shows up in a wheelchair, paralyzed. The perp is a white guy and somehow

Randall was able to keep any blacks off the jury. Randall gives the jury this sob story about how Ray ruined his client's life, accuses him of police brutality and hints that Ray's actions were racially motivated. All pure bullshit. The jury didn't buy it but Ray never has forgiven Randall for his tactics."

"I don't blame him," I said. "That's appalling." We finished up our sandwiches and I went back to the counter to get a coffee refill and two chocolate chip cookies. I gave one to Tommy.

"Thanks," he said. "What's new on your end?"

"Well, my love life seems to have taken a turn for the better." I grinned.

"That's not what I meant, and you know it," he said, also smiling. "You and Laura getting back together?"

"No. This is someone new, someone I just met a few days ago. She's a banker downtown. I think this has possibilities."

"Well, good for you. It's about time you settled down. I'd like to meet her. But I was asking about Susannah's case, wise guy." His demeanor became more serious. "Look, Alex, "I've lost some sleep over this. You told me Susannah wanted to talk with you about a legal problem, just before she was killed. You asked me to keep my eyes open for anything in the investigation that fit, but you wouldn't tell me what the problem was."

He ate the last bite of his cookie and looked me straight in the eye. "I don't want you out on a limb. The case against Bullard is taking on a life of its own. It's got nothing to do with any legal problem Susannah might have had. It's going to be very awkward if you come waltzing in with some new theory at this point – worse than awkward if you've been withholding evidence. What the hell are you up to?"

It pained me that I had put Tommy in an uncomfortable position, and I couldn't keep pushing him away. I also knew, from prior experience, that candid discussions with him frequently cleared my thinking. "Tommy," I said, "I'm between a rock and a hard place. I have an ethical obligation to keep what Susannah told me confidential, and beyond that, it would do a lot of damage if it became public. Furthermore, I'm not the only person with the information, and the others involved don't want it made public either. They are, however, in a position to help me uncover what, if anything, our information has to do with Susannah's death, and we've been working on it. At the moment, however, we've got nothing. Given Randall's stake in Bullard's conviction, he wouldn't give a damn if I told him what I know. My only chance of being any help to Susannah is to keep quiet and keep digging. I've got a few more rocks to turn over, and I should know more in a week or so. I know I'm putting myself in a tight spot, but I don't see any alternative."

"And what if you don't?" he asked. "Know more, I mean. Then what are you going to do? And if you do uncover something important to the case, aren't you just making it worse? You need an exit plan." We sat in silence for a minute while I pondered his questions. Sure enough, an idea occurred to me.

"Which judge was the Bullard case assigned to?" I asked.

"I don't know," Tommy said, "but I'll find out." He took out his cell phone and hit a speed dial number. "Hi Carol," he said, "it's Tommy. Can you transfer me to Jenny upstairs? Thanks." He waited. "Jenny, it's Tommy. Fine, thanks. You? Good. Listen, can you pull up the Bullard file and tell me who drew his case?" He waited. "Thanks a lot. Take care. Bye."

"Judge Callahan, Criminal Two," he reported to me. "Just got the case today."

"What do you know about him?"

"I had four or five cases in his court. Only one went to trial. He's been on the bench for maybe ten years. Impressed me as a solid judge; good common sense; not a grandstander. Had a reputation in the prosecutor's office as an even-handed guy, didn't tilt either way."

I considered this information and made a decision.

"OK," I said. "How about this? I'm going to look under the remaining rocks. When that's done, either way, I go to Judge Callahan. I tell him I have a question of professional responsibility related to the Bullard case. I say that I was waiting for the case to be assigned because I needed guidance from the presiding judge. If he agrees to handle it *in camera* and not bring in either the prosecutor or Bullard's lawyer, and I don't see why he wouldn't, then I'll lay my problem out for him. I'll tell him what Susannah told me and everything else I know. If he thinks it's relevant to the case, I'll ask him for an order releasing me from my confidentiality obligation and describing what I can tell Randall's office and under what conditions."

Hearing this, Tommy seemed visibly relieved. "Good boy," he said, as though I had just brought him a stick.

17

Driving back to the office, I reconsidered my thinking. I was warming to my spur-of-the-moment plan and didn't see any real flaws. There was the question of how to deal with the involvement of Morrie and Ellis, but maybe I could finesse that issue in talking with Judge Callahan. It seemed likely that he would buy my reason for not coming forward any sooner and overlook my subsequent intermeddling – particularly if I hadn't found anything – so it didn't seem likely that he would come down hard on Morrie or Ellis. There also was the question of whether the symphony's problem might become public as a result of my disclosure, but I was hopeful that Callahan would see the risk and require the prosecutor's office – and the public defender, assuming that's who was representing Bullard – to keep it confidential, at least for the time being. It didn't seem likely that Randall would take much interest in my story. Bullard's lawyer, on the other hand, was going to be all over it. An alternative theory for the murder was just what he or she needed. In any event, I didn't see that I had any viable alternatives. The next step was to bring Morrie and Ellis along.

I called Morrie when I got back to my office. He had an afternoon meeting at the Downtown Club and suggested that we meet there for drinks about five-thirty. I agreed and said that I would see if Ellis could join us. She could.

The setting sun was streaming through the floor-to-ceiling windows of the club's bar room when I arrived. Ellis was already there, sitting with Morrie. I joined them.

Morrie had with him Susannah's calendar, their telephone records, a banker's box containing her symphony files and her laptop computer.

My plan was to give Susannah's telephone records and computer to My Girl Friday. About two months ago our receptionist had called to tell me that someone was in our lobby asking to talk with Mr. Carrolton about a job. Her name was Friday, she said. I went out to the lobby, where I found a short, stocky, rather plain young woman dressed in a yellow outfit. She resembled nothing so much as a fire hydrant.

"Miss Friday?" I asked.

"It's Freitag," she said.

I shot a disapproving look at our receptionist who, despite her German ancestry, was under the impression that she had a sense of humor. She made a face at me.

"Priscilla Freitag. But Friday can be my job description. Your Girl Friday." I laughed. We sat down in the lobby and she gave me her resume. She was in her second year in the evening program at the downtown law school and needed a part-time job to help with her tuition. She had majored in computer science in college and wanted to be an intellectual property lawyer. Her resume was full of computer-related courses and activities and revealed that she knew several programming languages, most of which were acronyms that meant nothing to me. She also had a minor in library science and claimed to have outstanding research skills.

"Did you see *The Girl with the Dragon Tattoo*?" she asked when I had finished reading. "That's me, an overweight Lisbeth Salander. Only not so quirky. If you need someone to dig up stuff, I'm your girl."

"You're a hacker?" I asked.

She made a wavy motion with her hand. "That depends on your definition. Do you know what a 'white hat' is?" I didn't. "It's someone with my kind of skills who accesses other people's computers or systems, but doesn't do any damage. Looks for program weaknesses, security problems, that sort of thing. Usually under a contract with the owner. A felony conviction wouldn't look good on my bar application."

"You could access my firm's system?" I asked.

"Unless you've got state-of-the-art security, sure."

I knew that we couldn't keep Ms Freitag busy even on a part time basis, but I was intrigued by her skills and amused by her demeanor. I asked if she would be available for specific projects that might arise. She said she would. The big firms around town had their own information technology experts, and she was having no luck finding a more permanent relationship. Her current employment consisted of working a four-hour shift on the dishwashing line in the university cafeteria. We agreed on an hourly rate. I told I would check her references and that, if I was satisfied, her first assignment would be to test the systems at Carrolton Associates. She said she would send me an agreement to sign. Her references provided stellar recommendations. Within forty-eight hours of my returning her agreement, she reported back that she had found nine critical problems in our systems, fixed all of them, and included a detailed report of what she had found and a bill for her services. I sent her a check for the amount of her fee, plus a bonus.

The waitress arrived at our table in the bar and I placed a drink order. I told Morrie and Ellis about Ms Frietag's skills and our business relationship and my plan for the review of Susannah's records. I asked Morrie if he would approve the expenditure involved. He said he would.

"OK," I said, "Good. But let's think on down the road. We talk to Ann Conway, and we see what is revealed by Susannah's files. But if those are dead ends, what more can we do? Are there any other leads that we can follow? If not, then maybe we just have to pull back and hope that the symphony's auditors find our thief."

"You'll remember," Morrie said, "that Susannah wasn't sure the auditors would find the problem."

"I do," I said, "and I'm not happy with that outcome either. But I don't know where else we can go. And we may have only a limited amount of time in which to gracefully exit the scene. Here's what I'm thinking." And I went on to outline my strategy for approaching Judge Callahan.

When I finished, there was a lengthy pause while I sipped my drink and nibbled on some trail mix that the waitress had brought over. Finally, Morrie said, "OK. I see your point, and the plan makes sense. But I'm not agreeing to anything yet. I want you to finish with what we've got before we make any further decisions."

"OK with me, too," said Ellis.

18

I called Priscilla Freitag first thing the next morning. She said she could be at my offices at nine-thirty. In the meantime, I pulled up on my computer the contract form she had given me, made some modifications and printed out two copies. I also typed up a four page summary of what I knew related to my assignment from Susannah, who I had talked to and why, and what I had learned.

"Thanks for coming in so quickly," I said when Priscilla was seated in my office.

"That's part of being Your Girl Friday," she said, "not to mention the nice bonus. Thanks."

"You're welcome. I was impressed with your work. What I have for you this time is a little more complicated, but we need to cover a few preliminaries. You've had Legal Ethics?"

"Yes, last semester. I aced it."

"Then you know that legal assistants are bound by the same rules as the lawyers they work for."

"Right," she said.

"I'm acting in this matter as a lawyer, and the rules of client confidentiality apply. If you take on this assignment, I'll expect you to treat what I tell you, and anything else you learn, in the same manner. I'm not going to ask you to do anything unethical or illegal, but you have to agree that this won't go any further. Can you do that?"

"Geez," she said, with a touch of derision, "Just like those lawyer shows on TV!" Then, more seriously, "Of course I can keep a secret. I keep lots of secrets. You don't have to lecture me."

I thought about it for a minute, unsure whether I liked that response or her attitude. I decided that I did. Ms Freitag was no shrinking violet, and her assignment would require some independent thinking and a willingness to push the envelope. I picked up one of the documents I had on my desk and handed to her. "I've modified your contract form to fit the situation. Look it over, and if it's OK with you, sign it. Keep the second copy." She did.

"OK," I said, when she handed back the agreement. "I have a laptop that belonged to a woman named Susannah Townsend."

"The symphony lady? Who was killed a couple of weeks ago?"

"Yes. She was a client of mine. I don't represent her estate, but I am now representing her husband with respect to the same assignment that Mrs. Townsend gave me. It was Mr. Townsend who gave me her computer. Susannah had information indicating that someone was stealing from the symphony, and her husband found this in an envelope with my name on it after she was killed." I handed over a copy of the anonymous letter. Priscilla read it quickly.

I continued. "She wanted my help in finding out what was going on, and I think she had some additional information, but she was killed before she could give it to me and we haven't found it. What I want you to do is see if there is anything on her computer that relates to a theft or embezzlement from the symphony, and see whether her phone records tell us anything. Can you do that?"

"Cool!" she said. "Sure I can. But without knowing the cast of characters I may have some trouble connecting dots."

I handed over my summary. "This is what I know so far, including the names and relationships of the players. I didn't include the names of the symphony staff, but you'll see that I've also talked to each of them including John Martin, its CEO. Here's a list of those names." I passed over the document that Ellis had given me. "Ellis Kirkland is the symphony's treasurer and a board member. She and I conducted the staff interviews. We are scheduled to talk with Ann Conway, the former development director, tomorrow. I'll let you know what we learn from her. Also, I have Susannah's hard copy files related to her symphony activities. I'll be reviewing them and her appointment calendar, and I'll keep you advised of anything I find there."

"OK," Priscilla said, "This helps." She thought for a moment. "Aren't the police interested in this?"

"They're not," I said. "They have their motive and their suspect and the prosecutor's office isn't looking anywhere else. They did ask for copies of her phone records and calendar. All that is in the summary."

"Can I take this stuff home, or do I work here?" she asked.

"I'm going to set you up in a spare office down the hall," I said, "if that's OK with you. It has a computer with high-speed Internet access and a stand-alone printer. Will it slow you down if you're not working at home? I'd like to have your report by a week from today, at the latest. Sooner, if possible."

"No, that's OK. I live in the student apartments just over there." She pointed out the window. "I'm only a few minutes walk from here. I have classes most nights and my job at the cafeteria from eleven to three, but otherwise my days are pretty much free right now. Can I come in after hours? I can also work over the weekend."

I gave her a key to the offices. Since she already knew everything there was to know about Carrolton Associates, I didn't see any harm. I got her installed in her temporary quarters, introduced her to my assistant, showed her where the facilities and the coffee and soft drink machines were located, and left her to her work.

Back in my office, I opened the box containing Susannah's files. It occurred to me that this might not be all of her records, and that she could have put other files in storage. I could ask Morrie to dig them out, but the material in the correspondence folder dated back to January, so it seemed likely that what I had would cover the relevant time period. The other files were organized by subject matter – committees, personnel, special projects and so on.

There were several committee files. It appeared that Susannah sat in on a lot of meetings and took extensive notes. It also appeared as though she printed out and filed much of her e-mail correspondence, so I wouldn't have to rely on Priscilla for that piece. The thickest files were those related to corporate governance – policy issues, appointment of committees, recruitment of new board members and so on – finance, and fundraising.

I looked for a file with Ann Conway's name on it, and found one. I pulled it out. It appeared that Susannah had been careful about keeping the file materials in chronological order. Reading from back to front, I found a job description for the development director's position, Conway's application, her resume, an e-mail from John Martin containing some notes from her employment interview, an offer letter and acceptance, several performance reviews, and, in the front of the file, a single sheet of paper with notes in Susannah's handwriting, dated this past July. At the top of the page Susannah had written "Telcon with GA." The notes were cryptic, but included the words "Compromising position," "Won't say who," "Unacceptable," "Conflict of interest," and "Termination?"

Except for maybe the "conflict of interest" note, that all made sense in the context of what Ellis and I had learned from Josie Jackson. But the last notation on the page, around which Susannah had drawn a couple of circles, said "XYZ Trust??!!" I pulled out the file containing Susannah's fundraising materials and quickly paged through it looking for references to the XYZ Trust. I didn't see anything. There was no file with that name in the box. I thought for a moment and then picked up the phone and called John Martin.

"Hello, Alex," he said. "I was expecting to hear from you; if fact, I was intending to call you today. I've talked with Morris, and I'm afraid that I really can't tell you anything more about the Ann Conway matter." No surprise there.

"That's fine, John," I responded. "I understand. I was actually calling about something else. What do you know about the XYZ Trust?"

"The what?" He sounded genuinely perplexed.

"I've found a reference, related to the symphony, to something called the XYZ Trust. That name mean anything to you?"

"No," he replied, "it doesn't. Can you give me anything more to go on?"

"I can't," I said. "That's all I've got. You have some anonymous donors, do you not?"

"Well, yes," he replied. "Contributors who don't want their names used in our programs or for other public recognition. Of course, we know who they are. But we don't use code words to identify them. Internally, we refer to them by their actual names."

"Who, exactly, has those names?" I asked.

"Only me, the development department, and the chairperson – Susannah."

I thanked him and we hung up. I went back to Susannah's file on Ann Conway and looked at her performance reviews. After a reasonably good review following her first year, her evaluations had tailed off. Her salary increases for the past two years were almost flat. It was hard to know who was to blame for the symphony's fundraising problems, but I didn't get the impression that Ann Conway was part of the solution.

I walked down the hall and into the office now occupied by Priscilla Freitag. I gave her the XYZ name and asked her to be on the lookout for it. I also asked her to look for anyone who might be "GA" in reviewing the Townsends' telephone records. She wrote the letters and the date of the call on a legal pad. I noticed that she had made a lot of other notes. The office computer showed a blue screen with rows and rows of white letters and numbers, and she had Susannah's computer booted up in front of her.

"Anything interesting?" I asked.

"Not yet," she said. "Be a little patient, OK? I've only been at this for an hour."

Duly chastised, I slunk back to my office.

19

Ellis and I had made plans for an early dinner, as we had to be at the airport at six a.m. for our flight to New York. I was going to take her to Gino's. She had come downtown to run some errands and parked her car in the garage next to my office building. At five-thirty she was in my reception room and we went to my car.

"It looks like I'm not indispensable after all," she said after we were underway. "I just called my office and everything seems to be under control, but I'm going to have a lot of catching up to do when I get back. Being away for two weeks is hardly worth the effort."

"What do you usually do with your vacation time?" I asked. "When you're not playing detective."

"I travel some. I have a group of girl friends from college and we get together for a few days every year, usually in a nice place. I visit my folks. Nothing too exciting. What about you?"

"Well, when Laura and I were married and Becky was growing up, we rented a lake cottage for a couple of weeks in the summer, up in northern Michigan. I loved it there, and I still go back when I want to get away. Do some fishing, walk through the woods, read. The cottage comes with a small sailboat. I've sailed all my life. My dad taught me how, and I still love it. The owner and I have become friends and he doesn't rent to anyone else anymore, so the place is mine pretty much anytime I want it. He only uses it for a few weeks in the fall. Deer season."

"Sounds wonderful," Ellis said. "I'd love to see it."

I looked over at her. "I'd love to take you there," I said.

We arrived at Gino's. Gino Maretti, the founder, had died a few years ago and the place was now owned by his son, Paul. He greeted us at the door.

"Hello, Alex," he said, "who's this lovely lady?"

"Paul, meet Ellis; Ellis, this is Paul, our city's finest restaurateur."

"You are too kind. But, of course, it's true," he admitted. "This must be your first visit," he said to Ellis, "because I certainly would remember such an attractive guest." Paul was a good-looking young man, a second-generation Italian with old world charm.

Ellis blushed. "If flattery is part of your marketing plan," she said, "it's working."

Paul smiled and said, "I have your table ready, Alex. The best in the house. Follow me." He led us to a quiet table in a small alcove. We sat. Paul recommended that we try a new Chianti that had just come in, we agreed, and he left.

"I've had an interesting day," I said, and told Ellis about my meeting with Priscilla Freitag and my review of Susannah's files. I had made a copy of the page containing the notes of Susannah's telephone conversation with GA, which I pulled from my jacket pocket and handed across the table.

"This was in a file with Ann Conway's name on it," I explained. Ellis read it. "Any idea who GA might be?" I asked. She seemed not to hear. "Ellis?"

She started. "Oh, I'm sorry. No, I don't."

"Do you know anything about the XYZ Trust?"

She was quiet for a minute. "I..." she began, and then stopped. Finally, she said, "Do you remember our first meeting, in my office? You were dancing around the 'embezzlement' word, and finally asked if you could trust me."

"Yes, I remember."

"I said you could, and you can. But now I need to ask if I can trust you."

"Sure you can. But trust me to do what?"

"To keep what I'm about to tell you strictly confidential."

"OK," I said, "agreed." My curiosity was now on full alert.

"The XYZ Trust is a customer of my bank. It is very secretive. It does not want any information about its activities made public. We are not the only depositary for the trust's assets. It has banking and investment accounts with other financial institutions, but we understand that we are the lead bank. 'XYZ' is not its actual name, but that is how the account is known at the bank. I can tell you, as the bank's compliance officer, that this is all strictly legal, but I don't think I should say anything more. In fact," she added, "I don't know a whole lot more."

"Do you know why Susannah would have had the name? Or GA?" I asked.

"No," she said. "I'm surprised that she did. As I said, everything about the trust, including the fact of its existence, is a closely-guarded secret, at least within the bank. Susannah never mentioned it to me. But she was probably the most plugged-in person in town, and if anyone outside the financial community would know the name, it would be her." The grapevine again.

"What could the XYZ Trust have to do with Ann Conway?" I wondered out loud.

"I have no idea," Ellis said. "I was stunned to see its name in Susannah's notes. I can only assume that, in her mind, there was some connection between the trust and whatever it was that she discussed with GA."

I thought some more. "Don't we have to ask Morrie if he knows anything about the trust?"

"I guess we do," she said. "But we have to be careful how we handle it."

Paul returned with our wine, opened it, and poured a small amount into my glass. "I think you'll like this," he said. I did. "That's very good," I said. He filled our glasses and set down the bottle. "Tony will be waiting on you," he advised. "Here are the menus. Tonight's specials are at the top. I recommend the scaloppini." We reviewed the menus, Tony arrived, took our orders and left.

I said to Ellis, "Do we ask Ann about XYZ?" We talked about it. The only words in Susannah's notes that seemed outside the context of Ann's involvement in a messy love affair were "conflict of interest." That reference could infer that she also was a party to some improper financial transaction involving the symphony, but it just as readily might not. Laymen didn't always use that term the way lawyers did.

"I don't know," Ellis said, finally. "We have to be careful how we use this information. Let's see how the conversation goes."

"Let's talk about something other than the symphony," I suggested.

"OK," she said. "When can we visit your Michigan cottage?"

"Any time you want," I said. "But what say we solve Susannah's case first? Given our progress to date, I'm betting we can finish before deer season."

"When's that?" she asked.

"Late November, for firearms."

She groaned. "Being a detective isn't as easy as it looks on TV. They wrap up their cases in an hour."

Tony came by, noticed that our wine glasses were low, and refilled them. "Your meals should be out shortly," he said. He was back a few minutes later with two orders of the scaloppini, as recommended. It was excellent. We were just finishing dessert – tiramisu – when Ellis' cell phone rang. She pulled it from her purse and looked at the screen.

"It's John Martin," she said. "I wonder what he wants." She pushed the answer button. "Hello, John. What's up?" She listened for a minute, her face going white. "I see," she said. "Thank you for letting me know." And hung up.

"What's the matter?" I asked. It was several moments before she responded.

"Our meeting with Ann Conway is off."

"Why? What happened?"

"She's dead," Ellis said.

20

The call to Martin had come from the assistant to the CEO of the symphony where Ann Conway had taken her new job, Ellis said. The CEO was busy making calls to other members of the staff. All they knew was that Ann's body had been found a few hours ago behind a dumpster in back of the building where she lived in a fourteenth-floor apartment, having fallen, it appeared, from the deck of her unit. The police were investigating. No one had said if there was a suicide note or if foul play was suspected. Martin's source did say that Ann had seemed upset and distracted when she left work that afternoon.

Seated in my car in Gino's parking lot, Ellis and I called Morrie. She told him the news.

"My God," said Morrie. "That's a shock." There was a pause, none of us saying anything. Then Morrie articulated what each of us was thinking. "I have a bad feeling about this," he said. "Two women, both active in our symphony, die violent deaths within, what – two weeks? – of each other. What are the odds?"

Ellis shifted uneasily in her seat. "Have we stirred something up?" she asked. I had no answer to that. I couldn't discount the possibility.

"Morrie," I said, "I think we need to have a heart-to-heart talk with John Martin. We need to know exactly what happened between Ann Conway and the symphony. At this point, I don't care what her separation agreement says about confidentiality. And, unfortunately, neither does she."

"I agree," he said. "I'll call him right now and set something up for tomorrow. I'll call you back."

I started the car and headed back toward the garage where Ellis had parked. "Alex," she said, after a minute or two. "I don't want to go home tonight. I guess I'm scared. I know it's silly, but …." She looked over at me. "Do you have a room for me at your place?"

"Sure," I said. "You can use my daughter's room. It's all cleaned up. I can even find you a new toothbrush."

She seemed relieved. "Thanks. I won't be any trouble."

We had just arrived at my condo when my cell phone rang. It was Morrie. We had an appointment with John Martin for eight-thirty in the morning. "Morrie," I added, "one other thing. I've found a reference in Susannah's files to a trust account at Ellis' bank that seems to have something to do with the symphony. Do you know anything about that?"

"Not a thing," he said. I thanked him, and we hung up. "Nicely done," said Ellis.

I showed her around the place and got her situated in my daughter's bedroom. We got drinks and sat down in my study. It was then that Bruno made his entrance, cautiously stalking around the edge of the room toward my chair.

"Wow!" said Ellis. "That's a big cat!" Bruno stopped, looked at Ellis, sat down and started cleaning his face.

"His name's Bruno," I said, "but don't be offended if he keeps his distance, and I wouldn't try to pet him. He doesn't like strangers and can be a little aggressive." At which point Bruno stood up, walked straight across the room and jumped into Ellis' lap. "Oooff!" she exclaimed.

"Bruno!" I said, and got up to retrieve him. "No, no," Ellis said, "that's OK. I like cats."

"More amazing," I said, "he seems to like you. That's a first." Bruno lay down in her lap and closed his eyes, purring loudly.

We spent the next couple of hours talking about nothing much, avoiding Susannah and Ann Conway as topics of conversation. A little past ten Ellis announced she was going to bed, said good night, gave me a kiss and retired to her room. I logged on to the Internet, checked my e-mails and looked to see if there was anything further in the media regarding Ann Conway. The websites of the local New York TV outlets and newspapers were carrying the story, but it didn't seem to be front-page news. There was no further information about the circumstances of her fall. I sent an e-mail to Priscilla Freitag alerting her to Ann's death and attaching links to the news stories, and I asked her to pull up whatever she could about Ann's background. I pondered how this development affected the exit strategy that I had worked out with Tommy, and decided that, for the time being at least, it didn't. The phone rang. I looked at the clock; it was almost ten-thirty. I answered.

"Hi," said Laura. "I thought you'd be up. We haven't talked since the funeral, and I thought I'd check in and see how you were. Everything OK?"

I had not yet worked out in my mind how to approach Laura with my news about Ellis and my desire to bring an end to the relationship we had been sharing, such as it was. I was afraid that it wasn't going to be an easy conversation. Maybe now was the time to have it.

"Hi, Laura. Yes, I'm fine, thanks. You?"

"I'm very good, Alex, very happy right now, as a matter of fact." Pause. "Alex, there's no easy way to tell you this, so here goes: I'm getting married!"

I actually gulped. I hoped she didn't hear it over the phone. Recovering, I managed to get out "What…who…I mean, wow! That's great! Who to?"

"You don't know him. He's from Chicago. His name's George Westwood. We met at a convention about three months ago. He also works in the insurance business. He's a widower, a little older than I am, with two grown children. It all started out very low key, just acquaintances, then friends, then we had a few dates when he was here in town on business. And then, Boom! I'm in love!"

It went on downhill from there. Laura sounded like a schoolgirl. They were so happy together! He was just perfect for her! He was very successful! They were going to live in his big apartment in downtown Chicago! She hoped I would wish them well. Of course, I assured her. She'd tell me more later, she said, but right now she wanted to call

Becky. We rang off. Well, I said to myself, I can take that off my to-do list. I put our glasses in the sink, turned out the lights and went to bed.

I was just drifting off to sleep when I heard the door to my room open. I usually left the blinds half-closed because I liked having the lights from the city filtering in. In the dim light I could see Ellis standing inside the door. She had on a tee shirt that came down to her slim hips, and nothing else. Across the front it said "I Survived Three Mile Island – I Think". I remembered that Becky had brought it home from a high school party. I'd had to explain to her what Three Mile Island was. I hadn't seen it since. Except for the fact that she didn't have on three inch heels, it was hard to imagine a better way to display Ellis' long legs. My mouth went dry.

"Nice outfit," I croaked.

"I found it in the closet," she said. "I hope it's OK that I borrowed it."

"Fine with me," I said, drawing on my capacity for understatement.

She stood there, not moving. "I've been thinking about what we said the other night. About waiting."

"And?"

"If it's OK with you, I think we've waited long enough."

"Hmm," I said. "That phone call a few minutes ago?"

"Yes, I heard it ring."

"That was Laura. She's getting married."

We looked at each other, and both smiled. I silently thanked Laura for her exquisite timing and, with a clear conscience, pulled aside the bedcovers.

In the half-light of my bedroom, Ellis and I lay facing each other. The sheet, the blanket, my pajamas and the Three Mile Island tee shirt lay in a heap on the floor. There was just enough illumination to allow me to appreciate how finely put together her body was. She also knew how to use it. I reached over and stroked her hair.

"What made you change your mind?" I asked.

"About waiting?" she said.

"Yes."

She was quiet for a few moments. "I don't want you to think I'm a loose woman. Just the opposite. I'm afraid that my experiences with men have left me a little scarred."

"You were very young when you married," I said.

"Young and naïve," she said.

"But you were in love with him?" She thought for a minute.

"I think I'd say we were in lust, not love. We both had strict parents. Neither of us ever dated anyone else, and we didn't know anything about sex except that you didn't do it until you were married. We drove ourselves crazy, doing everything we could think of to each other short of intercourse – at least everything you can do in the back seat of a Ford Fairlane when you're almost six feet tall – and then feeling guilty about it afterward. The worst part was sitting in church the next morning, across the aisle from one another, listening to our pastor rant about the sins of the flesh. I felt as though he was looking straight at me. So, as soon as we could, we got married. So we could do it. And after we had done it, that was that. There wasn't anything else. I don't know that we really loved each other. We were too young. After he was killed…" She stopped.

"Well, suffice it to say that I haven't developed many relationships with men. Maybe I didn't trust my own motives, maybe I didn't trust theirs, maybe I wasn't ready for commitment. When I've tried, it's turned out badly. But, to answer your question, I've decided I can trust you. Not just to keep my secrets. Not to hurt me, I guess. Maybe even to protect me, if I need it."

Ellis Kirkland was vulnerable in ways that were shielded behind her no-nonsense business demeanor. "I'll do my very best," I said. And I meant it.

She turned onto her other side and drew her body up against mine. I pulled the blanket over us, put my arms around her, and we slept that way until morning – with one interruption.

21

The next morning, John Martin greeted Ellis, Morrie and me in the reception area of the symphony offices and led us into the conference room. Ann Conway's personnel file was on the table. Martin seemed nervous.

"This is very upsetting," he said after we were seated. "First Susannah, then your questions about Ann, and now she's dead too. Can you tell me what's going on?"

"John," I said, "I don't have any reason to think that these events are connected. We don't know that anything is going on. This is probably just a coincidence. But there's no reason, now, to hold back any information you may have."

"Shouldn't I be talking to the police?" he asked.

"Let's come back to that after you've told us what you know," I said.

He hesitated, looked at Morrie, and then tapped the file. "I'll make a copy of this for you, if you want it, but I don't think it will tell you anything you don't already know. The file doesn't show what really happened." He proceeded to tell us.

Susannah had come to see him in early August, very upset. She insisted that he not take notes of their conversation, so he hadn't. She said that she had received information that Ann was having an affair with someone in the symphony organization. She wouldn't reveal the source of the information, but she considered it reliable. She didn't say who the other party to the affair was and John had the impression that Susannah may not have known, but she did say he was married. She wanted Ann fired.

John suggested that Susannah was over-reacting; that sort of thing happens, after all; that it was a private matter between the participants; and that, without evidence of some harm to the organization, there didn't seem to be any reason to terminate Ann. Susannah had flared up. She told him that it wasn't just the affair; there was more to it. She wasn't going to say what – she indicated that it was highly confidential – but in her judgment Ann had to go, and that was that. Besides which, Susannah added, Conway was a lousy development officer.

John caved in. He wasn't going to get into a showdown with the chairperson of his board and the wife of the symphony's largest contributor, and he had his own doubts about Conway's performance. He told Susannah that he would take care of it, but that she had to let him manage the separation. He wasn't going to march in and tell Ann she was fired; it had to be handled with discretion if they were to avoid a possible lawsuit over wrongful termination. It wouldn't be wrongful, Susannah had said, not in her opinion. But John had pointed out that, based on what Susannah was willing to tell him, he didn't have grounds to terminate Ann for cause and that no one could predict what would happen – or what publicity might result – if she filed a lawsuit. He pointed out to Susannah that, if they were sued, she probably would have to go on record, under oath, with everything she knew. It was better, he argued, to find Ann another position and then let her resign. Susannah agreed this made sense.

As it happened, John had been aware through his professional connections of the job in New York, and it had been relatively easy to insert Ann into that position. They were glad to have her. The rest of the story – her termination agreement – was in the file.

"Tell us about your conversation with Ann," I said. "What did she say?"

"Surprisingly," he said, "it went pretty well. I reminded her that her performance reviews had not been very good lately, and said that we simply had to ratchet up our fundraising capability. I told her that I had lost confidence in her ability to meet our needs, and that key board members – I fudged a little and used the plural – shared my view. It was time to move on, I said, to a position that better matched her skills, and said that I was aware of an opening that might interest her. I'm not sure she bought this entirely, but she didn't argue. The rest of the conversation was about the new job possibility and what I was prepared to do to help her get it. She also insisted on an iron-clad confidentiality provision and a release of any claims against her as a part of her severance agreement. I agreed, on the condition that she would, in turn, waive any rights she might have against us. She agreed to that. The whole business took only a week and she was gone."

This seemed credible and it was consistent with what Josie Jackson had told us about Ann's departure. I looked at Ellis and Morrie, and neither of them seemed to have any further questions.

John then asked, "Well, do I talk to the police?"

I thought about that. It was possible that a report to Lieutenant Hammond of the story John had just told us wouldn't draw Hammond's attention to Ellis' and my investigation or Susannah's embezzlement concerns but, on the other hand, it might.

"Who would you talk to?" I asked.

"Why, the officers investigating Ann's death," he said. "The police here have Susannah's killer." Then a light went on, and he added, "Don't they?"

I didn't answer that question. "So your concern is that the information you have about Ann's affair might shed some light on the circumstances of her death."

He thought about that. "I guess I don't see what difference the affair makes," he said. "But Susannah seemed to think that Ann was involved in something improper, even if we don't know what it was. If her death was the result of foul play, then what I heard from Susannah might be relevant."

"It might," I agreed. "Why don't we wait and see what the investigation reveals as the cause of her death, and then decide what to do?"

John thought about that. He seemed to have forgotten his question about Susannah's case. He looked at Morrie. Morrie didn't say anything, but his body language was easy to interpret: Don't push it.

"OK," John said. "Let's do that."

22

Ellis and I went back to my office. Priscilla Freitag was there. Before introducing them, I warned Ellis that Priscilla could be abrasive and to not take offense at her demeanor. She really knows what she's doing, I said, even if she can't be taken out in polite society.

When they met, Priscilla seemed awed by Ellis, who towered over her. For once, she made no wisecracks and was actually civil. I had the sense that, when reincarnated, Priscilla would happily give up her technical wizardry in exchange for Ellis' good looks. Walking back down the hall, Ellis said, "That wasn't what you lead me to expect. She seemed very pleasant."

"I don't know who that woman was," I said, "but it wasn't the real Priscilla Freitag."

I got us some coffee and we sat down in our conference room with Susannah's files and appointment calendar. We agreed that Ellis would begin with the calendar, as she was more familiar with Susannah's activities and contacts, and I would continue to review the files. I went to the front of the box and pulled out the correspondence jacket. Starting in January, I began working my way forward in time. I had reviewed January and February when Ellis said,

"Here's something interesting. On March 22 Susannah met with the senior trust officer at my bank. Morrie has several of his business accounts with the bank, but he and Susannah aren't personal customers of ours. I wonder what that was about."

"The XYZ Trust?" I suggested. Ellis thought.

"Well," she said, "that would explain how the name could appear in the notes of her conversation with GA. He certainly knows about XYZ."

"Can you ask him about it? What's his name?"

"Gordon Parker. So how does that conversation go? 'Gordon, in my spare time I've been poking around looking for Susannah Townsend's killer, and the trail leads straight to you.'"

"Hmmm," I mused. "Not bad, but let's call that Plan B. Couldn't you just say that you had been going through some of Susannah's symphony records, found a reference to the trust and were wondering if he had any idea how she knew of it? Wouldn't he be the logical person to go to with that question?"

"Well, yes," she said. "When we were setting up the XYZ account and sorting out all the legalities, he was the point person from our trust department. I would guess he knows as much about the trust as anyone at my bank. But it's a long shot. We're not the only financial institution that does business with XYZ. There are three or four other places in town that could have been the source of Susannah's information."

"Let's think about it," I suggested. We went back to our respective tasks. I worked my way to the front of the correspondence file without seeing anything of interest and started in on the project files. I pulled out the fundraising materials, which I had quickly scanned the day before, and went through them more carefully.

What I found were agendas of meetings of the symphony's development committee, minutes of the committee's meetings and notes in Susannah's own hand. The materials dated back three years. Their general tenor confirmed what Ellis had told me in our first meeting: that the level of annual fund contributions was declining and that the symphony's endowment wasn't large enough. There had been many discussions about how to attack these problems. The development committee was close to making a recommendation to the board of trustees that the organization launch a major endowment campaign. Consultants had been brought in to assess the feasibility of doing so, and were supportive of the plan. There was concern that an endowment campaign would do short-term damage, as it was likely to dilute contributions to the annual fund, but there was no real choice. The future of the symphony, the committee believed, could be assured only if it controlled its own destiny and reduced its dependence on current contributions. The only missing piece, in the judgment of the committee, was some compelling incentive – maybe a matching commitment from a lead donor – that would fire up the prospective contributors. This situation must have been very much on Susannah's mind as she grappled with the embezzlement disclosure.

Ellis was carefully going through Susannah's appointments but not finding much. There were many names with which she was not familiar and notations that didn't make any sense to her. She thought the engagements related to the symphony were consistent with what we already knew, at least insofar as she recognized the names. She found the appointment with John Martin at which they probably had their conversation about Ann's termination. Susannah's appointment with Harvey Anderson and her appointments with me were the last that seemed to have any bearing on our problem. For three o'clock on the afternoon of the day she was killed, her calendar said only "Symp. mtg. here."

I thought about that. If the meeting was just between her and me, wouldn't the notation have been "Mtg. with Carrolton" or something like that? "Symp. mtg." seemed to suggest that it was going to be more than just the two of us. I asked Ellis about it. She agreed.

Having spent the night at my place, Ellis hadn't had a change of clothes since the day before, and she wanted to go home and freshen up. She said that she was sure she would be OK. She had set the burglar alarm when she left her house, and it was broad daylight. She was feeling better about things, now that the initial shock of Ann Conway's death had worn off. But would I like to come to her place for dinner...and spend the night? Sure I would, I said. I had sandwiches brought in for lunch and we ate in my office, after which she left. I spent the remainder of the day completing my review of Susannah's files, but I didn't find anything that shed further light on our questions.

On the way out of the office, I stuck my head in the room where Priscilla was working.

"Patience!" she said, before I could get a word out. "I might have something for you soon. I'm going to be here over the weekend, so just relax." Back to her normal self.

I went home, fed Bruno, left him some extra food, threw a change of clothes into a small duffle and left for Ellis' house.

23

As it turned out, I spent the weekend. Ellis was an excellent cook, and we had some great meals. On Saturday night we went to see a movie. We talked. We made love. I finally left for home after dinner on Sunday. Ellis thought she might do some shopping on Monday and we agreed that she would come for dinner at my place that evening. She would do the cooking, she said, and was going to pick up what she needed for the menu she had in mind. I protested, but not too vigorously. My culinary skills were pretty limited.

Priscilla Freitag was already there when I arrived at Carrolton Associates on Monday morning and she followed me down the hall to my office, carrying a folder with some papers in it. I had learned not to ask about her progress, so we both sat down and I waited for her to begin.

"I think I'm done," she said. "I was here most of the weekend. I'm sorry I can't stretch this out – I could use the money – but you said you were in a hurry. Let's start with Mrs. Townsend's computer.

"First, her hard drive had nowhere near the amount of data that you'd find with an average user. She wasn't one of those people who keeps everything on her computer. So there wasn't much to look at and I didn't find much. The letters XYZ don't appear together in any of her files or in any e-mails, in- or out-bound. Whatever she knew about the XYZ Trust didn't make it to her computer. So I can't help you there. There was a lot of symphony stuff. Letters, memos, e-mails…a lot. I ran several algorithms on those files trying to find word patterns that might add up to something about embezzlement, theft, fraud, et cetera. Nothing.

"I also tried to connect the names Ann Conway, Ann and Conway to anything in her files that might help us. There were a number of hits on the name, but nothing connecting it to anything interesting. It's my conclusion that whatever she knew about that anonymous letter, or about Ann Conway, was in her head or written down somewhere else."

I guess I was disappointed and it showed.

"Hey," Priscilla said, "I'm sorry, OK? But I can't make something out of nothing. Oh, one more thing. In late July Mrs. Townsend ran some Internet searches looking for information on embezzlers. It looked like she was trying to figure out how they did it. She wasn't very good at using search engines, but she found several web sites on the subject. If she read them, she would have had a pretty good understanding of how embezzlers operated. At least some of the common techniques."

"OK," I said. "What else?"

"Ann Conway," she said. "I spent some time on the net looking for more information on her. Some of it was pretty interesting. For example, did you know she had a criminal record?"

"What!"

"Yeah. But not under the name Conway. Her real name is Merton. Anne – with an 'e' – Merton. She was convicted of being an accessory to an extortion plot in Nevada eight years ago. She turned state's evidence and got off with time served."

"How on earth did you find…" She cut me off.

"Look, do you want me to spend the time that it would take – a lot, by the way – to explain to you how I do it, or do you want the facts?"

"Just the facts, ma'am," I said. I congratulated myself on the subtle allusion to Joe Friday and its clever tie-in to Priscilla's surname, but she didn't get it. Probably a generational thing, I thought.

"OK," she said. "Then listen and don't ask a lot of questions. Your Ann Conway is really Anne Merton. She was born in California, went to UCLA, dropped out during her sophomore year, held a couple of jobs – one of which was with a fundraising consultant – and then got an associate's degree in something called 'public administration' from a two-year college in Texas. She married a guy named Peterson but she kept the name Merton. She worked at nowhere jobs in Texas for a couple of years, divorced Peterson, and moved to Nevada. She got lucky in Reno and landed a job in the development department of the University of Nevada.

"To make a long story short, it appears as though she got hooked up with some low-life who persuaded her that it would be a good idea to shake down one of the university's big benefactors. Using her access to the school's contributor data, Merton – or Conway – gave her boyfriend a name and some personal information on the guy. Well, as you might expect from amateurs, it blew up in their faces. The info they were going to use against their mark was already public. He went straight to the cops and they nailed both Anne and her friend. She spilled her guts and he got five years."

"Question?"

"What?" she snapped.

"How do you know that Ann Conway is really Anne Merton?"

"That's the first thing I found," she said. "She filed in Nevada state court to change her name, after the conviction. Conway was her middle name; she just dropped 'Merton' and the 'e'."

I opened the box containing Susannah's files and pulled out the Ann Conway folder. I took out her resume, which contained no mention of Nevada, and gave it to Priscilla.

"Look at this," I asked. She did.

"A lot of this is BS," she said, "and it sure isn't the whole story. The stuff about the other fundraising jobs she held between Nevada and coming here is right, more or less, but I really didn't dig that deep. It looks like she had enough experience to talk a good game. If you want, I could check up on the people she lists as references, look into their creds, check the 990's of her employers, things like that."

"Let me think about it," I said, making a mental note to have a conversation with John Martin about the symphony's due diligence procedures. "Tell me about the phone records."

"Not much to tell there, either." Priscilla said. "I ran all the names you gave me against the Townsend's land line and her cell phone records. There were several hits. I've listed all of them." She fished in her folder and handed me a two-page print-out, stapled at the top. She had provided the dates of the calls, the call duration, the name of the caller or person called and the other party's telephone number.

"This stuff is publicly available?" I asked.

"No," she said. "Some I got using the Townsends' account numbers, but some I had to – uh – coax out of the phone company's computers. Since it was the Townsends' data I figured no one would mind."

"What about GA? Any guesses?"

"Take a look at the date on Susannah's notes of that conversation." I did. There were two calls listed. One was with Sara Atkins, whose name I remembered from our staff interviews. She worked in the symphony's accounting department. The other was with Harvey Anderson. No GA.

"Well?" I asked.

"Well nothing. Those were the only conversations that day with people on your list whose last names begin with A. I got no ideas. Maybe Mrs. Townsend wasn't using her own telephone."

I picked up Susannah's appointment calendar and turned to the day of the call. She had several appointments that day and had been in and out of her house. It was certainly possible that the conversation with GA had been on someone else's phone. She had spent some time at the symphony offices; maybe the call took place there. Dead end.

"Priscilla," I said, "You've been great. Very impressive. There's one more thing I'd like you to do. Stay on the investigation into Ann Conway's death and let me know what you find out. And send me a bill for your services to date."

"OK," she said. "Here's a report on what I found and some printouts that you might want to look over." She gave me the folder she had brought in. "Let me know if there's anything else."

She stood up, thereby increasing her elevation by about ten inches. "By the way," she said, "you're not the first guy to hit me with that lame Joe Friday line."

24

Talking with Ellis that evening over dinner at my place – she had prepared lamb chops, one of my favorite dishes – I briefed her on what I had learned from Priscilla Freitag. She was stunned to discover that Ann Conway wasn't who she had represented herself to be. She was beginning to have doubts about John Martin's leadership, she said. Conway's hiring had been his decision.

We discussed the lines of inquiry left open for us. It seemed to me that the only avenue holding any prospect for further information was Gordon Parker, the trust officer at Ellis' bank. Maybe he was the source of Susannah's information about the trust, and maybe, just maybe, he would reveal the link – if there was one – between the trust, Susannah, Ann Conway and the symphony. If a conversation with Parker didn't produce something worth pursuing, then I probably would have to call Judge Callahan and see if we could engineer a graceful exit from our situation. Ellis agreed.

We considered how to approach that conversation and whether there was some way to include me. Given the sensitivity of the XYZ Trust to any dissemination of information about it, it was going to be hard enough for Ellis to get Parker to discuss the subject with her, let alone with me in the room. On the other hand, it seemed disingenuous for Ellis to have a conversation with Parker that he would assume to be private and among co-workers, and then tell me what she had learned. Our best idea was that Ellis would ask for the meeting, tell Parker that Morris Townsend had engaged me to represent him in connection with a matter related to Susannah's activities, and that

I would be there. That should at least get me in the room. If Parker balked when we mentioned the XYZ Trust, we would just have to see how much he was willing to tell us.

Ellis was to make that call in the morning. We finished off our dinner with a dab of peppermint ice cream and coffee. "Tell me," Ellis said when we had moved into my study with refills of our coffee, "how you feel about Laura getting married." I thought about it. Other than having acted as a catalyst for getting Ellis into my bed, I hadn't assigned much importance to the news. I wasn't surprised at her decision, I said. Laura wasn't the type to live alone and enjoy it. She needed a man around, and I knew I wasn't that man. I hoped she would be happy. I was more concerned, I said, about Becky and how she would react. I was surprised that she hadn't called me after talking with her mother.

"They have a close relationship?" she asked.

"Yes," I said, "they do. But I think that Becky has given up on the possibility that Laura and I would get back together. She seems to have understood that better than I did. Laura's decision to marry someone else will probably be upsetting to her – the finality of it – but that's part of growing up. Things change."

"When you do talk with her," Ellis asked, "what are you going to say about me?"

"Actually," I said, "that part should be pretty easy. Becky has told me more than once that I should find someone and settle down."

"Oh?" said Ellis. "Are we settling down?"

I immediately regretted my choice of words. "I'm sorry," I said, "I didn't mean to suggest…"

She laughed. "No, really, I'm glad it came to mind." Then she became serious. "I don't want to push you into anything, Alex. I'm happy to be with you, that's all, and I'm looking forward to seeing how this all works out."

"Exactly how I feel," I said. She came over and sat in my lap. One thing led to another and before long we were back in my bed.

Ellis had the foresight to bring along a change of clothes, so she spent the night. We left for my office after breakfast the next morning. Ellis would call Gordon Parker from there. We agreed that she should press for a prompt meeting, today, if possible. I thought back over the timeline of my involvement with the Townsends. It was now more than two weeks since Susannah's death and five days since Judge Callahan got the Bullard case. We really did need to wrap this up.

Fortunately, Parker was available for a meeting that afternoon. Ellis spent an hour looking through the materials that Priscilla had assembled while I attended to other business. We had a late lunch at the Downtown Club and, at the appointed time, rode the elevator down to the floor on which Gordon Parker's office was located.

We met in a conference room. Parker was in his late fifties or early sixties, probably nearing retirement. He was an academic type, nearsighted, with thick glasses, balding, unkempt, and with a slightly distracted air. I envisioned his office strewn with files and loose paper. Ellis had said that, while he knew his business, he could be a little disorganized. After introductions and the initial pleasantries, we came to the point of our visit.

As he knew, I said, I was representing Morris Townsend. The matter was confidential and I wasn't at liberty to disclose its nature, which I was sure he would understand, but it related to Susannah's work with the symphony. That was why Ellis was involved, in her capacity as the symphony's treasurer. Harvey Anderson, the symphony's legal counsel, also was aware of my engagement, I said. I hoped he wouldn't pick up the phone and call Harvey, and he didn't.

"Morris has given me some files that Susannah kept, and her diary," I continued, "and the diary shows that she had a meeting with you on March 22. I also discovered in her papers a possible reference to something that transpired in that meeting. An understanding of what was said in the meeting could be important to my inquiry, and I'm hoping that you can tell me what the meeting was about."

"I know exactly what that meeting was about," Parker said. "It's also confidential." The tenor of his response suggested that, in his view, our conversation was at an end.

I plunged ahead anyway. "Susannah's notes contain the name XYZ Trust," I said. "That's what I'm interested in. I know from Ellis that your bank has a relationship with the trust, but that's all she would tell me. I have given her my word that this information will go no further, and I will give you the same assurance. I also can tell you that Morris Townsend seems to be unaware of the either trust or his wife's relationship to it – if there is one. Whatever is said here can stay in this room."

Parker shot a look at Ellis and she stared right back. "I guess you know what you're doing," he said. "You're the bank's compliance officer. What can I say?"

"Gordon," she said, "I only know about the structure of our relationship with the trust. I have no knowledge of its terms or what would be in its best interests. That's going to have to be your call, but you know that Morris Townsend's company is a major customer of ours and I can tell you that this is very important to him. If there's some reason why we can't answer Alex's question, it had better be a good one."

Parker waivered. I could see the wheels turning in his mind. He took off his glasses, wiped them on a handkerchief and, in the process of putting them back on, stuck one of the temple pieces in his eye. He hardly seemed to notice that misstep and, after a few moments more he said, "OK. I'm going to take you at your word that this won't go any further. Most of what I'm going to tell you will become public in a few months anyway. But you've got to keep this quiet until then." We nodded.

"This is a little complicated, so bear with me," he began, in his best professorial manner. "The bank is a depositary for what we are calling the XYZ Trust. The grantors of the trust are the children and grandchildren of – well, you probably can guess who, so I'm not going to use his name. His estate was finally settled last year and distributions were made to its beneficiaries. For tax reasons, the family beneficiaries – all of whom were very well off even before the testator died – agreed that the major part of their inheritances should go to charity, specifically, to our major local arts organizations. They formed the trust to act as the vehicle for this purpose."

I was sure that I knew who the testator was: Henry Tichner. Henry was the son of Emanuel Tichner, the founder of what was now the largest publicly-traded company in town, and had assumed leadership of the enterprise when his father died. He built it into a manufacturing powerhouse and greatly increased the value of its shares, of which he owned a large number. Henry was over eighty years old when he died and a little eccentric. Henry's lawyer was one of his contemporaries, a nice old guy but probably not conversant with the intricacies of the federal estate tax. Or maybe Henry didn't like the plan his lawyer suggested and simply refused to follow it. Whatever the reason, the buzz around the local tax bar was that the government was going to be the principal beneficiary of his estate unless some very creative post-mortem planning was done, and fast. It seemed likely that what was being described to us by Gordon Parker was the result of that effort.

"We use 'XYZ' as the name of the trust," he continued, "in order to protect the identity of the benefactors. They want to keep their involvement confidential and they don't want any publicity. When the trust's activities are eventually made public, their role will be acknowledged but in a way that focuses on the testator and deflects attention from them. And, in the meantime, they don't want to be lobbied by all the other charities in town whose names aren't on the list.

"The March 22 meeting was a private introduction of the trust to its major beneficiaries – the symphony, the art museum, two of the local theater companies and three of the smaller museums. They won't get the same amount, but each institution is going to receive a substantial sum. The benefactors want to have a game-changing impact on a few institutions rather than spread the funds over a large number of charities. The gifts will be unrestricted, so each beneficiary will be able to use the funds however it wants. We thought we should give them a heads up as to what was coming their way, so that they could plan accordingly.

"The only people invited to the meeting were the board chairs and chief development officers of the beneficiary organizations. Susannah was here along with the symphony's development person. I don't remember her name. We met in this room. They were all asked to sign a confidentiality agreement and I then described to them the reason for the meeting and the objectives of the trust. I passed out envelopes containing an estimate of what each could expect to receive. There would be three distributions, one in each of the last three quarters of the year, to smooth out market fluctuations, and I warned them that the distributions might not be in equal amounts. The board chairs and development officers would be notified when those transfers were made, and of the amounts. The distributions would be deposited in an interest-bearing agency account here at the bank that we have set up for each of the beneficiaries, and then those deposits would be transferred to the institutions after the final trust distribution was made in December.

"I emphasized that they were not to make any public statements about the gifts until the agency accounts had been closed and the trust had issued a press release describing its actions, and that there would be limits on what they could say. They would receive further information on this point. They were told that their gifts might be in jeopardy if they failed to follow any part of my instructions.

"Needless to say, the audience was giddy with excitement. There were some questions, most of which I refused to answer, and the meeting adjourned." He stopped.

"Why weren't the beneficiaries' chief executives invited to the meeting?" I asked.

"The CEO of one of the beneficiaries has a reputation for loose talk. We couldn't risk including her, and we couldn't invite all of the other CEOs and not her. We wanted a high-level staff person there, so we settled on the chief development officers. We felt they might be more attuned to the need for confidentiality in donor relationships and better accustomed to following orders. After the meeting I pulled aside the board chair and development officer of the institution in question and emphasized that they were not to put their CEO in the loop. I assume that, despite my instructions, at least some of the CEOs now know what's going on, but as far as I know there have been no leaks. It goes without saying that the beneficiaries have a significant incentive to do as they were told."

I looked at Ellis, but she didn't seem to have anything to say. I felt that we had what we had come for and thanked Parker for his cooperation.

"There's something else you might want to know," he said. "Susannah called me some time after the first distribution was made. Early July, I think. She had received the notice of the deposit in the symphony's agency account and she wanted to confirm that it had received the correct amount. I looked up the amount transferred to the symphony and told her that it had. She then asked me what was the total amount deposited in all of the beneficiary accounts. I didn't see any reason not to tell her, so I did. She thanked me and hung up."

"What was the amount of the symphony's distribution?" I asked.

"Seven million, seven hundred fifty thousand dollars," he said. I could see why the beneficiaries had been excited, and I could easily imagine Susannah's delight in considering how to incorporate what might amount to a twenty five million dollar windfall into the symphony's fundraising plans. This news would have fit perfectly into the development committee's thinking about an endowment campaign. Her concerns about urgency and secrecy in the handling of her suspicions also were apparent. She couldn't risk a disclosure that might jeopardize the gift from the trust.

As we stood to leave, one additional question occurred to me.

"You said that the bank is a depositary for the trust. Who is the trustee?"

"The sole trustee is the lead lawyer for the family," he said. "For the reasons I described, the family also wants him to keep a low profile in this matter. That's why I have been handling the relationships between the trust and the beneficiaries. You mentioned his name earlier. Harvey Anderson."

I thought about that. "Did Susannah know Harvey was the trustee?" I asked.

Parker frowned. “That’s the strangest part,” he said. “She called me later and asked who the trustee was, and I told her. That was the day she was killed.”

25

I walked Ellis to her car and she drove home. I had a dinner engagement with a prospective client from out of town, set up two weeks ago, so Ellis was going to spend the night at her place. Back at my office, I settled down with the brief I was working on. My intention was to concentrate on something else for an hour or two and let what I knew about the Townsend case settle in my mind. But my thoughts kept coming back to what Gordon Parker had told us.

We had been pursuing the suspected embezzlement for two reasons: first, to ascertain whether the symphony had been the victim of a theft and, if so, to restore any loss; and second, as a path to the discovery of who killed Susannah: find the theft, find the thief, find the killer. So what did we now know about the theft? Several pieces of the puzzle seemed to be coming together.

First, there was, in fact, a reason why the XYZ Trust and Ann Conway would have been linked in Susannah's mind. Second, there was a lot of money involved in the symphony's relationship with the trust, which fit with Susannah's statement to Ellis about the size of the suspected theft. Third, Conway knew something that no other symphony employee did. The classic embezzler is someone in a position to take advantage of special knowledge, and Ann fit into that category. Fourth, someone – GA – had reason to think that Conway was acting improperly, maybe illegally, and that information convinced Susannah to get rid of her. Fifth, someone had sent Susannah an anonymous letter suggesting embezzlement. Did all of this add up to Conway being a thief? And a killer?

I picked up a pencil and wrote these thoughts on a legal pad. I sat there, staring at my notes. What was I missing? Finally, I focused on GA. Who was he? Or she? Where did he get the information that he passed on to Susannah? Why didn't a name with those initials turn up in Susannah's telephone records? Now that everyone carried a cell phone in his or her pocket, it seemed likely that, if Susannah had made the call, she had used hers. And wasn't it more likely that it had been an incoming call? Maybe Susannah had called GA and they had been talking about something else when the subject of Ann Conway came up, but there was a higher probability that that GA had called Susannah.

I put the phone call aside and turned my thoughts to the anonymous letter. Was GA also the author of the letter? Or was there a second person who suspected that Conway was stealing? Both were possibilities, but I started with the assumption that GA and the letter writer were the same person. Was there any reason to think that Conway was the "boss?" Not literally, as there was no one in the symphony organization with the initials GA and our interviews had not suggested that the letter had been written by anyone on the staff. But that didn't rule out the possibility that Ann was the letter writer's target.

Where did the letter fit in the sequence of events? Was it sent before or after Susannah's conversation with GA? If the letter came first, then maybe the call was an escalation of GA's efforts to get Ann fired. Or it could have been the other way around: the call hadn't had the desired effect, so GA followed up with the letter.

The other possibility was that the "boss" and Ann Conway were not the same person. Under this scenario, the letter writer could have been tipping off Susannah to something completely unrelated to Conway's activities. If this was the case, then it seemed doubtful that GA was the author of the letter. But nothing in what we had learned so far suggested that Susannah thought there were two different embezzlements. So, I concluded, based at least on what we knew, my first assumption was correct: GA and the letter writer were one and the same and Ann Conway was the target.

I mulled this over for several minutes. And then I had another thought. GA's conversation with Susannah and the facts reported in the letter could be alluding to the participation by two different people in the same criminal act. Maybe we should be looking for conspirators. The phone call from GA implicates Ann, and the letter points Susannah toward her partner in crime. So perhaps there were two whistleblowers, each seeing the same events from different perspectives. But it also was possible that GA had facts implicating both and was acting alone.

Then another piece of what we knew about Ann came bubbling up. Her legal problems in Nevada had emerged out of a love interest. Susannah had told John Martin that Conway was having an affair with someone at the symphony. Had that relationship also evolved into a criminal enterprise? Thinking back over what John had told us about his meeting with Susannah, it seemed probable she thought so.

OK, so I hadn't found the theft, but I had a plausible theory as to who the thief was – or at least one of them. If I could figure out who Ann was having the affair with, then I might have two. And I might know who the killer was.

My thoughts then turned to another question. If Susannah was right, and if Ann Conway had been having an affair with someone at the symphony, why hadn't we heard anything about it from the symphony staff? In my experience, people who worked together in an office environment were pretty well attuned to that sort of thing. Of course, Ellis and I had been asking them about thieves, not lovers, so personal relationships might not have been top-of-mind for the people we interviewed. I didn't relish the idea of going through another round of staff interviews in which the subject would be the love lives of their co-workers. And, thinking back on Ellis' descriptions of why we were there, I could recall that she had alluded to personal relationships as one area of interest under the whistleblower policy. My best guess was that, if there was an affair going on, no one at the symphony knew about it other than the participants. And GA.

That brought me back to the phone call. I pulled out the folder containing Priscilla Freitag's report and found her summary of the

Townsends' telephone records. Two hits on last names beginning with A on the date in question – the conversations with Sara Atkins and Harvey Anderson. I put aside the fact that the first initial G didn't match up with either last name. I checked the organizational chart that John Martin had given us. As I had recalled, Atkins worked in the accounting department, so she would not have reported to Conway. And I remembered from our interview with her that she was fairly new to the staff. She had been very convincing in her denial of any knowledge about matters covered by the whistleblower policy. It seemed unlikely that she would have had the facts reflected in Susannah's notes of the conversation in question.

That left Harvey Anderson. As the symphony's legal counsel, there was nothing noteworthy in the fact that he had talked with Susannah, the chairperson of the symphony board, on this or any other day. They probably spoke on a regular basis. And while he had a connection to the symphony, I couldn't see how he would have come into possession of information about Ann Conway's love life. Nor could I imagine Harvey as the whistleblower. He had available much more effective means of bringing any legal concerns to the symphony than writing an anonymous letter or tapping into Susannah's grapevine.

I stared at the list of names and numbers. Then, suddenly, I got it.

26

My dinner engagement with the prospective client went very well. I was hired to pursue a Tax Court appeal of an IRS deficiency determination against his software company amounting to almost eight hundred thousand dollars. If I was successful, the fee arrangement we agreed upon would provide a nice boost for the revenues of Carrolton Associates. I thought the case had real possibilities and I was looking forward to digging into the facts and the law. When they're not crime-solving, tax lawyers can get excited about stuff that would bore others to tears.

It was only nine o'clock when I got home, so I called Ellis. She was watching a chick flick on TV, she said, and missing me. I missed her too, I said. Were her doors locked, I asked? Yes, she said, they were. Good, I said. Don't let anyone in unless it's me. She laughed. Was I coming over? I thought about it and said yes, I was. I could review with her my thinking about the case, and there were other benefits to not sleeping alone at home.

As I was preparing to leave, my phone rang. I assumed that it was Ellis, perhaps changing her mind. But, when I answered, it was Becky. She wanted to talk about Mom, she said. How did I feel about her getting married? I said I was happy for her, and had wished them well. I asked what she thought. Her reaction was pretty much what I had described to Ellis.

"I'm not surprised that you and she didn't get back together," she said. "I gave up on that a long time ago. I could see that you weren't happy together. This George guy sounds all right. But I'm not going to call him Dad."

I laughed. "You'd better not!" I said. "Uh, look, Becky," I continued after a brief pause, "I have some news along the same lines."

"Don't tell me you're getting married! Are you trying to freak me out? One parent at a time, please!"

"No, no, not that," I hastened to add. "But I have met someone that I like, a lot, and we've been seeing quite a bit of each other. But we're not about to rush into anything." I went on to tell her about Ellis, stopping well short of any intimate details. I knew what TMI meant, and besides, it was none of her business.

"I'm anxious for you to meet," I said. "I think you'll hit it off. And here's the clincher: Bruno likes her!"

"OMG," Becky replied. "Bruno doesn't even like me!" We chatted some more, and I found an opportunity to ask her about Nina. Had they talked recently?

"Yes," she said. "Just yesterday. She seems to be getting along, adjusting to life without her mother. It's very hard for her. They were close."

"I'm sure it is. Did she say anything about the police investigation?"

"Only that the detective in charge had called maybe a week ago to see if she remembered anything more about her conversations with her mother. She said she didn't. He seemed like a nice guy, she told me, and was really interested in the case. But she didn't have anything to add to what he already knew. Oh, and he also asked if she had heard her mother talk about a woman at the symphony named Ann Conway. I remember the name because one of my freshman roommates was named Conway. Anyway, Nina told him that she had heard her mother mention the name, but didn't know anything more. She wondered why he was asking but then, a few days later, she saw in the newspaper that an Ann Conway, who used to work for our symphony, had died in upstate New York. Nina thought that was creepy."

So Lieutenant Hammond was inquiring about Ann Conway before she died. Interesting.

"Yes," I said, "I was aware of that," but I didn't say more. We chatted a little while longer, talking about her school work, how she liked this semester's classes, her professors and so on. Things seemed to be going well. I thanked her for calling, told her I loved her, and we hung up.

It was late when I arrived at Ellis' house, the movie had just concluded and she was weepy, but she quickly recovered her composure and laughed at herself. "Movies usually don't affect me this way," she said. "Maybe I'm a little wrought up over everything that's been happening – Susannah, Ann, you, me – everything."

I raised my eyebrows. "Oh, don't get me wrong," she quickly added. "I'm happy with you, with us. That's not it. I'm just sorry that we haven't made more progress. I feel that justice for Susannah is slipping away, out of our hands."

"Well," I said, "I think I may have some answers. For starters, I think I know who GA is."

"How did you figure that out?" she asked.

I reminded her of Priscilla Freitag's research into the Townsends' phone records and the conclusion that Susannah had only two conversations on the date in question with people whose last names began with A. We could rule out Sara Atkins. That left Harvey Anderson. The insight that had come to me as I stared at Priscilla's report was that the number listed for the other party to that conversation was not Harvey's office number. The prefix was from an area on the north side. I had gone to my computer, done a reverse look-up, and discovered that the number was that of Harvey's residence. Harvey's wife was named Virginia – probably known to her friends as Ginny. GA was Mrs. Harvey Anderson. The conversation hadn't been with Harvey; it had been with his wife.

"Her nickname is Ginny, all right," Ellis said. "I know her, but only slightly. We've talked at symphony events." She thought for a few moments. "But we still can't prove that Conway is the thief and, if she is, we don't know what she did."

"You're right," I said, "and Ginny may not know either, but our next step is to talk with her."

Ellis thought she could set up a meeting with Ginny without raising an undue amount of curiosity on her part. She would call tomorrow and make the arrangements.

27

Ginny Anderson turned out to be a redhead with an attitude. She arrived at Ellis' office at two o'clock the following afternoon. In their phone conversation that morning Ellis had been vague about the purpose of the meeting, saying only that it was important. I was seated in Ellis' office when she escorted Ginny in, and I stood and introduced myself. Ginny was a fading beauty, probably spectacular at one time but now a little overweight and shopworn. I told her that I was a lawyer representing Morris Townsend, and that the reason for the meeting with her was to ask her some questions about Susannah and the symphony.

"God, that poor woman!" Ginny said, as we sat down. "But I hardly knew her. Whatever it is you're looking for, I'm not going to be able to help you much." This line almost sounded rehearsed, and I could sense her drawing into a defensive mode.

"Actually," I said, "our questions are fairly specific. We found a note in Susannah's files of a telephone conversation with you back in July. We're hoping that you can tell us more about what you discussed."

"I'm not sure I remember that," Ginny answered, warily.

"It had to do with Ann Conway," I reminded her.

"What the hell's going on here?" she snapped. "I don't have to talk with you about that! What are you up to?"

"Are you aware that Conway is dead?"

"Yes, of course. I read the papers."

"There is an on-going police investigation into the cause of her death. We're not involved in that, but the circumstances may touch upon matters of interest to the symphony. We thought it might be productive if we could discuss this informally, just among ourselves, without bringing in the police."

That comment had the desired result.

"The police!" she exclaimed. "I don't have anything to say to the police!"

"Well," I suggested, "then let's us just talk about it and maybe it won't be necessary for this to go any further." She sat there sullenly, trying to make up her mind how to handle us.

"What do you want to know?" she demanded, finally.

"First," I said, "did you tell Susannah that Ann Conway was having an affair with someone at the symphony?"

She thought about that for several moments, suggesting that she was going to carefully weigh each response from now on.

"Yes," she said.

"Did you tell her who the other party to the affair was?"

Pause. "No," she answered.

"Do you know?"

She hesitated again. "Yeah, I know," she said.

"Who was it?"

"None of your business," she snapped.

"The cops investigating Ann's death are going to think it's their business," I suggested.

Something flashed across Ginny's face, as though she had just made some heretofore unseen connection. Was it fear? Concern? Whatever it was, she quickly suppressed it and recovered her combative attitude.

"Then let them ask me," she said.

I thought about that for a moment. "OK," I said, "let's move on. Did you tell Susannah that Ann was stealing from the symphony?"

"Yes, I did."

"How did you know that?"

At this point, Ginny Anderson got up from her chair. "OK," she said, "that's it. I'm out of here."

"Ginny," Ellis said, "listen. You're leaving us with no alternatives. If we can't talk this through and understand what happened between you and Susannah, the next step is that you're going to be dealing with the New York police. If you won't talk to them, you're going to be charged with obstructing justice. You can't just walk away from this."

Ginny teetered unsteadily for a second or two, then collapsed back into her chair and burst into tears. She wept uncontrollably for several minutes, her body shaking. Between sobs, I could make out, "…never gotten involved…such an idiot…so mad at him...just had to get even…Now look what I've done."

She calmed down after a few minutes, and then the floodgates opened and it all poured out. Ginny had come home a day early from a visit to her sister's and found Harvey and Ann in bed together. Her own bed! Ann was unperturbed. She got up, gathered up her clothes, walked naked into the bathroom, got dressed and left. Harvey went on offense, accusing Ginny of snooping around and deliberately trapping them. She knew the marriage was over, he claimed, although according to her she knew no such thing. She thought everything was just the way it had always been. She didn't want a divorce and he didn't ask for one, but he wouldn't agree to stop seeing Ann either.

This standoff went on for a couple of weeks with no resolution. That was when Ginny took matters into her own hands. She called Susannah and made her allegations about Ann's affair, being careful not to say who with, and hinted at some type of wrongdoing on her part. She hoped that Susannah would believe her and get Ann fired, out of town and out of her life. What she said about the other party to the affair having a connection to the symphony was true, she rationalized. She needed to get Susannah's attention, and Harvey was the symphony's lawyer.

But, Ginny reasoned, the affair might not be enough. She had to drive a stake through Conway's heart. She had no facts to support her suggestion that Ann was involved in a theft from the symphony, but

Susannah didn't ask for any. But when the phone call didn't produce any immediate results, she got the idea of writing the anonymous letter, thinking that Susannah would view it as supporting evidence. She figured that Susannah would assume that Ann was the "boss," since Ginny had planted the thought that she was a thief, and probably would think that the letter was independent corroboration of that conclusion. At least that's the way Ginny tried to make it look.

Listening to this explanation, it occurred to me that there were two things Ginny didn't know, both of which had worked in her favor. First, Susannah had lost confidence in Ann's abilities as a development director and, given the pressure she was under to improve the symphony's fundraising, didn't need much of a push to fire her. Second, at the time Ginny placed the phone call, Susannah was puzzling over the distributions from the XYZ Trust and was primed to believe that someone might be stealing from the symphony. Ann was the only other person at the symphony with knowledge of the XYZ relationship. It was easy to move Susannah to the conclusion that Ann was somehow involved in malfeasance, even if she didn't know what or how.

Ginny went on to say that Ann's death had been a horrible shock. Even a slut didn't deserve to die like that. It had scared her.

"Why?" I asked.

"I don't know, really," she said. "I just have this feeling that all of this is connected – her affair with my husband, my getting her fired, what happened to Susannah, and then Ann…it's just spooky. I didn't want her dead, just out of the way."

She looked at me and then at Ellis, with something approaching fear in her eyes. "Please," she said, "don't tell Harvey that I've talked to you."

28

The next morning, I had just sat down at my desk when my phone rang. I answered.

"Alex," a male voice said, "this is Harvey. How are you?"

"I'm fine, Harvey," I said. "What can I do for you?" My first thought was that he had somehow found out about my conversation with Ginny and was calling to excoriate me for questioning his wife about his extracurricular love life. But that wasn't it.

"I was just checking up on your progress with Susannah's problem," he said. "How's it going? Anything you can tell me?"

There was a lot I could tell him, but I wasn't going to. "Well," I said, "I've talked to people at the symphony, but I haven't come to any firm conclusions. There's still a lot I don't know."

"I understand," he said. "You know, I've been thinking about what Susannah told me, and it really doesn't make a lot of sense. We may never know what she was worried about. I'm afraid I've sent you on a wild goose chase. If I were you, I'd close my file and let the symphony's auditors handle it. What else can you do?"

"I'm not sure," I said. "But if I do get to the bottom of this, I'll let you know."

We said goodbye and hung up. So now Harvey was telling me not to waste my time on Susannah's concerns. Quite a shift in his attitude since our conversation at the county club.

Within thirty seconds, our receptionist called. There was someone here to see me, she said. A policeman. He wouldn't give her his name.

I walked out to the lobby and there was Lieutenant Ray Hammond. I said hello. Can we talk for a minute? he asked. Yes, I said, certainly, and led him back to my office.

We sat down and he looked around the room. I had the impression that he didn't miss much. "What can I do for you, Lieutenant?" I inquired, wondering what the hell was going on.

"I'd prefer it if you'd call me Ray. This isn't an official visit. May I call you Alex?"

"Please do," I said.

"Tommy Glynn says that you're a straight up guy," he continued, "and that you can be trusted to keep your mouth shut. Is that right?"

I considered what else Tommy might have told him, but quickly concluded that I could rely on his discretion. "Yes," I said. "It is. At least I like to think so."

"OK," he said. "This is just between you and me. All right?"

"Sure," I said. "Understood."

"I hear through the grapevine that you've been talking with people at the symphony about Ann Conway. I'm curious how you got there, but let's leave that alone for now. I thought you ought to know that the New York cops think she was murdered. They're pretty sure it wasn't suicide. I know this because I asked. They hadn't made any connection between her death and her job here. I called them. And here's where it gets a little tricky." He stopped.

I briefly contemplated how he might have learned of my inquiries at the symphony but concluded that, as Susannah so well knew, the grapevine spread everywhere. His news about the cause of Ann Conway's death, while not totally unexpected, would require some digestion. Hammond looked me in the eye and, apparently satisfied, continued.

"The Townsend case is, for all practical purposes, closed and I have no official interest in it any longer. We're going for a conviction of Albert Bullard. So my being here and talking with you is off the record. But, as you probably know from Tommy, I'm not convinced we have the right guy. But if it's not Bullard, then who is it? You tell me you are working on a legal problem for Mrs. Townsend. Mrs. Townsend had a lot of interests and knew a lot of people, but the symphony got most of her attention. You're not her regular lawyer. Is the legal problem a symphony problem? Then I hear you're interested in Ann Conway. Then Conway winds up splattered on the pavement behind a dumpster in upstate New York, also murdered. And I'm thinking that maybe Conway and the legal problem are connected. And if they are, then is Conway's death somehow connected to Townsend's?" He paused.

"Am I making any sense?" he asked.

He was, in my opinion, making a lot of sense. But all this was happening pretty fast, and I wasn't sure how much I should disclose. I also remembered what Tommy had told me about Hammond's opinion of Steve Randall. The thought crossed my mind that Hammond might be looking for some way to embarrass Randall, and I didn't want to get involved in a personal vendetta of his. So I just answered the question in front of me.

"Yes, I think you are," I said, putting the ball back in his court.

Ray was quiet for a few moments. "Look," he said, "I can see why you would be uncomfortable here. You've got to think about your professional responsibility to Mrs. Townsend. I'm not trying to trip you up and I'm not asking you to reveal any confidences. But if you know anything that might help me out, we could be sparing an innocent man a lot of grief."

I thought some more. I was impressed with Hammond. He obviously was running some risk to his career by talking with me and continuing with his inquiry into Susannah's murder, worried about convicting the wrong guy despite the official position that the case was closed. If his motives did include taking Randall down a notch, he nonetheless had come to some solid conclusions about what was going on in Susannah's case. A good cop, like Tommy had said. I decided to cooperate, as far as I could.

"Ray, you may be right," I said. "I can't tell you everything I know, at least not at this point. But I can tell you this. Conway was fired from the symphony and it was Susannah Townsend who caused that to happen. I've also discovered that Ann Conway is not her real name and that she had a criminal record. She turned state's evidence and agreed to plead guilty in a Nevada state court to being an accessory to an extortion scheme. She was born Anne Conway Merton – Anne spelled with an 'e' – but changed her name following the conviction."

He almost smiled. "I'm impressed," he said. "You've got some good sources of information. I know about Nevada. The New York police ran Conway's fingerprints through the FBI database. But I didn't know about her being fired. What more can you tell me about that?"

I felt that I could add one additional piece of information. "Conway was having an affair with someone in the symphony organization," I said. "That seems to have been an element in the decision to let her go." I wasn't sure that I should reveal the name of the other party to the affair, so I didn't.

Ray considered that news. "Hardly seems like a reason to fire her," he said. "That stuff happens all the time. There's got to be more to it."

I wasn't sure how to respond. "You said we are off the record," I said. "Am I correct in assuming that this conversation isn't going to wind up in a report somewhere?"

"Look," he said, "we each have our reasons for keeping this low key, at least for now. I'm not going to go running to Steve Randall with what I learn here. But I've got to tell you, if any of this leads to a change in our view of the case, then you're going to have to go on the record with what you know."

It was at this point that an idea occurred to me. If the circumstances were presented to Judge Callahan in the right way, there might be a chance we could maintain the confidentiality of Susannah's information while, at the same time, getting Ray Hammond into the loop and keeping Randall out. He and I spent the next half-hour working through my thinking. Then I called Tommy and told him what Ray and I had agreed on.

"OK," Tommy said. "Good. I like it."

Ellis and I met Morrie for lunch. We briefed him on our meeting with Ginny Anderson. He was stunned to learn that Ann's paramour was Harvey Anderson. None of us liked the implications of this development. And I told them about the call from Harvey. After we had discussed all of this for several minutes, I said I thought it was time to implement our exit strategy and let the police take over.

Morrie didn't like that idea. The fact that I had no theory as to how an embezzlement had taken place didn't improve his confidence in my judgment. Some thoughts regarding this question were beginning to take shape in my head, but I wasn't ready to roll them out.

"You saw what happened with the investigation into Susannah's death," he went on. "You know how invested Randall is in a conviction of Bullard. What makes you think that Harvey Anderson's peccadillos will get him to re-open the investigation?"

"I agree that's not likely, based on what we know." I said. "But there's been another development that, I think, plays into our hand." And I went on to tell them about my conversation with Ray Hammond, my conclusion that he was someone we could work with, and the strategy we had agreed on. "If this works," I continued, "and I admit it's a big 'if' because it all depends on Judge Callahan, then we accomplish several objectives: we get ourselves out of the line of fire, we get the police involved on a discrete basis, we keep Randall out of the loop for now, we maintain the confidentiality of the situation at the symphony, and we have good reason to believe that Hammond will take what we know and run with it.

"And here's the best part," I went on. "If whatever Hammond turns up comes to Randall under a court order, he'd have to take it seriously. He'll be obligated to turn it over to Bullard's lawyer, and he would know that the defense is going to use it at the trial. It puts Randall in the position where, if his evidence doesn't completely dispose of the new facts, then Bullard's lawyer is going to use it to beat him about the head and shoulders."

"Reasonable doubt, ladies and gentlemen of the jury, reasonable doubt!" I pontificated. "You must consider all of the evidence. Think about the possibility that Susannah Townsend was killed by the perpetrator of some massive embezzlement from the symphony. Why does the prosecutor want to sweep this under the rug? My client is innocent!"

"Even I could probably get an acquittal," I concluded.

Morrie thought about this for several moments. "OK," he said. "Good. I agree."

29

I went back to my office and Ellis went home. She had only two days of vacation time left and wanted to drive upstate and visit her parents. She thought she would leave that afternoon, spend three nights and come back on Saturday. I promised that I would stay in touch.

At nine-thirty the next morning I was seated in Judge Callahan's chambers. I had called him as soon as I returned from my luncheon meeting with Ellis and Morrie. The case the judge was trying had just settled, his secretary reported, and his calendar was clear for the remainder of the week. I took the first available time.

Callahan looked as though he had been sent over from Central Casting. Tall, abundant white hair, long white moustache, blue eyes, big-boned. His right hand engulfed mine when we shook. Deep, gravelly voice. I liked him immediately. We sat down. His chambers were orderly, no files stacked on his desk or credenza. Surprisingly, the bookshelves were devoted to literature, histories and biographies and not to volumes of case reports or criminal law treatises. His robe was hanging on a coat rack near the door.

"What can I do for you, Mr. Carrolton?" he asked.

"Judge," I began, "this meeting relates the Albert Bullard case. I understand that it has been assigned to you."

"That's right," he intoned.

"I am a member of the bar of this state. Shortly before her death, the victim in the Bullard case, Susannah Townsend, engaged me to represent her in a legal matter. Under an express pledge of confidentiality on my part, she gave me some information that directly related to that engagement. I now believe that the information in question could be relevant to the state's case against Mr. Bullard. I also believe that the information is privileged and that I am ethically bound to maintain its confidentiality. I am here seeking your advice, as the presiding judge, as to what, if anything, I should do with what I know. I am hoping that you will consider this as an *in camera* conversation and that you will not find it necessary to include the prosecutor's office, or Bullard's defense counsel, until you have heard what I have to say and made a decision as to how to handle it."

His eyebrows went up and he looked at me over the tops of his glasses. Anticipating his next question, I continued. "I've been waiting for the case to be assigned so that I could speak with the presiding judge."

"That was a week ago," he said. His tone was non-judgmental, but there was a question implicit in the comment.

"Your honor," I said, "The facts here are complicated, and I have been uncertain as to the exact boundaries of my confidentiality obligation. Over the past several days I have been making some inquiries in an effort to put what Mrs. Townsend told me into context. I now believe that I can present the issues to you in an orderly way."

"Mmm," he said. He thought for perhaps thirty seconds. "All right," he said, "I understand. But allow me to decide how to address the issues. As you can appreciate, we are on delicate ground here."

"Certainly, your honor," I responded, although I had been hoping that I would be able to lead him to the outcome I had in mind.

"First," he said, "do you represent Mrs. Townsend's estate?"

"No, I do not. After Mrs. Townsend died, her husband, Morris Townsend, asked that I continue with the assignment his wife had given me, and I now represent him. I have his consent to talk with you."

"So Mr. Townsend is aware of the information given to you by his wife? The information you say is privileged?" I confirmed that was the case. "And he learned that from you?" I nodded. "Didn't that disclosure violate your professional responsibility?"

"Yes," I confessed, "it might have, but there are other facts to consider. Given the possible relevance of the information to the circumstances of his wife's death, I felt that Mr. Townsend had a right to know what she had told me. Also, before making that disclosure, I had discovered that there were two other persons to whom Mrs. Townsend had given the information in question before she came to me. Those also were confidential conversations, and those persons and Mr. Townsend have agreed to not disclose what they know."

Judge Callahan held up his hand. "All right," he said, "that's enough for now. Let me digest this." He stood up, walked across the room and stared out the window, thinking. I remained seated. After a couple of minutes he returned to his desk and sat back down. I had the distinct impression that I was at a watershed moment. What transpired in the next few minutes could very well have me on my way to a disciplinary proceeding.

"I have a few more questions," he said. "But when you answer, I don't want you to tell me anything about the substance of the information in question. I only want to hear it, if I ever do, in the courtroom, on the record and as a part of the evidence in the case. I appreciate how you have handled this conversation so far."

That sounded good. Maybe I was going to skate through this. "Yes, sir," I said, "I understand."

"First," he said, "who is the executor of Mrs. Townsend's estate?"

"Her husband, Morris Townsend."

"And he is now a client of yours, but not in his capacity as executor, is that right?"

"Yes, your honor." He thought about that for a few moments.

"Second, would the release of this information cause any damage to Mrs. Townsend's interests? By that I mean her personal financial or reputational interests."

"No," I answered.

"Would it be damaging to any third party that Mrs. Townsend would have a natural interest in protecting? Her family, for example?"

"Yes," I said. "That was her principal reason for insisting on its confidentiality." He thought about that. It seemed as though he was about to pursue this line of questioning, but then decided not to do so.

"Third, you said that the information could be relevant to the Bullard case. Can I take that to mean that, in your opinion at least, the interests of justice might be served by the introduction of the information in question into the evidence stream?"

"Yes," I said, "I believe so."

"Hmm." He paused again. "Do you have any experience in law enforcement, Mr. Carrolton?"

"Yes, your honor. I spent eight years with the FBI as part of a financial crimes unit after I graduated from law school. In the course of that work I investigated and prepared cases for trial."

Judge Callahan thought for another minute and then said, "All right, Mr. Carrolton, you seem to have given the circumstances a lot of thought. Do you have a recommendation for me as to how I might handle this?"

"Yes," I said, "I do."

30

I left Judge Callahan's chambers with a confidential order that he had entered in the Bullard case. He had sealed the order and its contents would not be given to either party unless he later determined to do so. He would make that determination if and when the need for further action became apparent. The judge also reported to me that Bullard was now represented by a lawyer from the public defender's office, and he said that he would advise both her and the prosecutor's office of the existence of the order but not its content. The order described what I was to do with what I knew but, consistent with Judge Callahan's interest in protecting the record in the case, I had not revealed that information and the order did not discuss it. I was to report back to the court once I had complied with its terms.

My meeting with Callahan hadn't gone as I had expected, but the outcome was exactly what I had hoped for. He had adopted – with a few minor modifications – my recommendations as to how to manage the disclosure of what Ellis and I had discovered and he seemed willing to overlook any possible transgressions of the code of professional responsibility on my part. Of course, he didn't know how I had handled the original police investigation, so I wasn't entirely clear of an obstruction of justice charge, but I thought that I had effectively mooted that risk. For the first time since Susannah's death, I was optimistic about how things were going. That was to be short lived.

As I was driving back to my office my cell phone rang. I answered. It was Priscilla Freitag.

"Carrolton," she said, "someone is trying to hack into your system."

"What? How...? Are you talking about Carrolton Associates?"

"Yeah," she said. "Every couple of weeks I've been running follow-up checks on the work I did for you, just to make sure everything was still OK. I did another one this morning. It looks to me as though, about one a.m. last night, somebody tried to access your data. They seemed to have a particular interest in the Townsend matter, judging from the queries."

"Did they get anything?" I asked.

"No, of course not," she responded. "When I fix something, it stays fixed. I just thought you ought to know."

"Is there anything further we should do?" I asked.

"Nope," she answered. "Just another service of Your Girl Friday."

"Thanks, Priscilla," I said. "You're the best." And we hung up. I had a bad feeling about this development and, after thinking for a minute, decided to alter course and head for home. Call it a premonition. When I got off the elevator on my floor, standing in front of the entry to my unit was a man that I recognized as an employee of the building management firm. He was the guy who usually attended our condo association annual meeting to report on issues related to the maintenance of our building. The door to my unit was standing open and it looked as though the lock had been forced.

"Ah, Mr. Carrolton!" he said, when he turned to see who had exited the elevator. He had out a cell phone. "I was just calling my office to get your cell number. We've had a little problem here. One of your neighbors called to report that your door had been damaged. I just happened to be on the premises so I came up to see what was going on."

Seeing that I couldn't come up with his name, he stuck out his hand. "Lou Baldwin, from Excel Property Management. I've seen you at the meetings."

"Yes, Lou, thanks. I remember you. Did you go inside?" I asked.

"No," he said. "Just got here."

"You haven't seen my cat, have you?" I asked. "Big, brown male with black stripes?"

"No. But he couldn't have gone anywhere unless he got a ride down on the elevator."

I started through the door.

"Uh, you might want to stay out here," Lou advised. "We're probably looking at a crime scene."

"I'm sure we are," I responded. "I'm not going to touch anything. I just want to find my cat. Can you call 911 for me?"

"Sure," he said, and did.

I stepped into my hallway. The living room seemed to be untouched, as did my bedroom and the guest bedroom. I continued up the hall. The kitchen didn't seem disturbed, but when I looked into my study, it was a mess. "Bruno?" I called. No answer. Not good. He usually came to greet me whenever I arrived home. I stepped into the room. My desk had been ransacked and my laptop computer was gone. A credenza where I kept file material had been opened and the files dumped out.

Then, over against the far wall, I saw him. Bruno was lying on the floor, not moving. I stepped over the intervening mess and knelt down beside him. There was blood coming from his mouth. My first reaction was that he was dead, but then I could see that he was breathing shallowly.

"Aw, Bruno," I said. "Who did this to you?" I pulled out my cell phone, looked up the number of his veterinarian, and punched the call button.

"Central Animal Hospital," a voice answered. "How may we help you?"

"This is Alex Carrolton," I said. "Is Elsie in? I have an emergency."

"I'll put you right through," the voice said.

"This is Elsie, Alex. What's going on?" I described to her what I had found.

"Don't move him," Elsie Follen said. "I'm coming right over. I'll be there in ten minutes."

I moved back into the hallway. "I'll go downstairs and show the police in," Lou Baldwin said. "I'll have someone here to fix your door within two hours." He handed me a card. "Here's my number if you need me." He hadn't been gone more than three minutes when the elevator doors opened and two uniformed policemen stepped out.

"Mr. Carrolton?" one asked. "Yes," I answered. "Look," I said, "I've been inside but I didn't touch anything. My cat is in there, badly hurt. I've called the vet and she should be here any minute. I've got to get her in to see him. He's in the study, and that's where all of the damage is."

"OK," the older cop said. "Let us clear the place and make certain no one is in there, and then we can wait for the vet. Just tell her not to touch anything."

"Thanks," I said. "Another request. Could you please call Lieutenant Ray Hammond, give him my name and address and tell him what's going on here? I'm sure he'll be interested."

"OK," he said again, and got on his radio. He and his partner then went inside. Just as they returned to the hallway, having found no one, Elsie showed up with one of her assistants, each carrying a bag of equipment.

"Where is he?" she asked, with no preliminaries.

"The study," I answered. "Try not to touch anything. There's been a break-in. That's why the police are here." I led them to where Bruno was lying and they both went to work. I couldn't see what they were doing but after a few minutes Elsie said, "OK. I think I have him stabilized. We're going to have to get him back to our place so we can get some x-rays and do lab work. I think some ribs are broken. There may be internal injuries. It doesn't look good, Alex. He's hurt pretty bad."

"Do whatever you can for him," I said. "And don't worry about the cost."

Her assistant extracted a small folding stretcher from one of the equipment bags, unfolded and locked it in place, and she and Elsie carefully slid Bruno onto it. Elsie had inserted an IV into Bruno's leg and her assistant was holding up the fluid bottle. "Here," she said to me. "Hold this for a second," and handed me the bottle. She and Elsie then lifted Bruno up and, as they got him clear of the wall and debris, I could see that there was blood on his front paws and hair stuck in the claws. I pointed it out to Elsie. She looked and said the hair wasn't

Bruno's. I called to the senior policeman, still standing in my hallway, and asked him to bring in some evidence bags. They put the stretcher down on my desk and, using tweezers, Elsie carefully pulled the hair from Bruno's claws, then took a swab and gathered up some of the blood. The cop bagged the samples.

"Attaboy, Bruno," I said. "At least you got a piece of him."

31

Lieutenant Hammond showed up about half an hour after Elsie left with Bruno, accompanied by a woman he introduced as Detective Liz Jordan.

"I've told Detective Jordan everything she needs to know about our situation here," Hammond said to me, with a look that made it clear that I shouldn't volunteer anything further. "She's going to look around and see what she can find." He surveyed the damage to my study. "No other rooms were disturbed?" he asked.

"No," I answered.

"Let's go in another room," he suggested, "and let Liz get to work in here." We moved into the living room. When we got there, I said, "It's pretty clear that they were looking for information. I don't think they took anything other than my laptop and maybe some papers. I'd have to sort through my files to see what might be missing."

"What did you have on the laptop?" he asked.

I thought about it. "Other than my personal stuff, there were some e-mails about the Townsend case and some files containing symphony records – financial statements, that sort of thing. Nothing that important."

"Tell me about the e-mails," he said. "Who with?"

"We'd better sit down," I said. "This is going to take a while." We sat, and I told him what had happened in my meeting with Judge Callahan. Then, acting in accordance with the terms of the judge's order, I proceeded to tell Hammond everything I knew, or suspected, about the possible embezzlement at the symphony, Susannah

Townsend's actions, her conversation with GA and her identity, the anonymous letter, Ann Conway's involvement with Harvey Anderson, what I had learned about the XYZ Trust. I went on to describe the roles that Ellis Kirkland, Morris Townsend and Priscilla Freitag had played in my investigation.

As I had suggested to Judge Callahan, his order required that everything I had just disclosed to Lieutenant Ray Hammond, the principal investigator in the Townsend case, was to be kept in strict confidence by him and used only in connection with his continuing investigation into the murder of Susannah Townsend, pending my report back to the court and the judge's further determination as to its disposition. The judge had given me a letter addressed to Hammond in which he had said just that. I took the letter out of my pocket and handed it to him. He read it, and smiled. "Nice work," he said. "Nothing like having the law on your side."

"One other piece of news," I said, and told him about the attempt to hack into my office computer system.

"OK," he said," so the hacking and the break-in here are part of an attempt to find out what you know about the Townsend case, and whoever took your computer knows – or soon will – that you are conducting an investigation of some sort and that Kirkland, Morris Townsend and Freitag are helping you."

"Yes," I said, "but they wouldn't learn much else. The interviews that Kirkland and I had with the symphony staff weren't exactly a secret. They'll find out that Freitag was doing some background research but they won't know what she found. They won't discover my suspicions about the identity of Conway's co-conspirator or the involvement of the XYZ Trust, because there was nothing about either one in my computer. And the computer was password-protected, if that makes any difference."

"Probably not," Ray said. "But it might slow them down."

He thought for a couple of seconds and then asked, "Where is Miss Kirkland now?"

"Visiting her parents, upstate. She's coming home on Saturday."

"Where does she live?" he asked. I told him.

"I'm going to send a black and white out there," he said, "Just to check things out." He pulled out his cell phone and made the call. "I don't really have an excuse to set up surveillance," he added.

"I can probably work something out," I said. "Mr. Townsend's company has a private security force that looks after its properties. I'll ask him to put someone on watch at Miss Kirkland's house for a couple of days if she wants it."

"Good," Ray said. "Do that. And it wouldn't be a bad idea to have some security here in this building."

"I'll talk to the management," I said. "And I'm going to hire someone to sit in the lobby at my offices for a few nights."

"That leaves Ms Freitag."

"She lives in the student apartments near the campus," I said. "I would imagine that the building has some sort of security on a regular basis. I'll call her and tell her what's happened here, and make sure that she'll be OK." I thought for a moment. "Are we over-reacting?" I asked.

"Better safe than sorry, as we say in law enforcement," he said.

Detective Jordan stuck her head in the room and announced that she was finished. She had picked up some fingerprints that probably would turn out to be mine, but she would check them out anyway. The best bet for identifying the perpetrator, in her opinion, was the hair and blood samples that Elsie had taken off Bruno. Did Hammond want to authorize the expense of a DNA test? After all, it was only a break-in. Yes, he said, he did. "What do we have for a matching sample?" she asked. "Nothing, yet," Ray said. "In the meantime, we'll run the results though the FBI database and see if we get any hits."

He and Liz Jordan left and, as they did, two men showed up with a new door. "You're in luck," one said. "We found a match in storage in the basement. Otherwise, we'da hadda put up some piece a junk until we cudda had one made." In about forty-five minutes they had switched my lock and had the new door installed. It needed painting but I was again secure. Or at least as secure as I was when I left this morning. Which is to say, not very.

While they were working on the door, I made calls. I reached Ellis, Priscilla and Morrie and told them what had happened. Ellis said not to bother with security at her place; she was staying with me when she returned. And she had her computer with her. Was Bruno going to be all right? I had to tell her that I wasn't sure, but that Elsie was going to do everything she could to save him and she was a great vet.

Priscilla confirmed that her building was protected with both a card key system and a night watchman, and she had no concerns about someone getting into her apartment. Just let 'em try, she said. Since I had her on the phone, I asked if there was anything I could do about the information contained in my stolen computer. "I use a logon password," I reported. "Will that keep them out of my files?"

"No way," she responded. "Passwords only keep out people who follow the rules. Anybody can get his hands on a password cracker. You can download them off the Internet. Would take about ten seconds."

"Do you save your passwords for sites you visit on line?" she asked. I did not, I said. "Are you sure?" she pressed. "What about your e-mail? Do you re-enter your password each time you log on?" I didn't. "Then it's saved," she said. "Change it right away." I don't have a computer, I pointed out. "OK," she said. "I've got your address; what's your current password?" I told her, and I could hear her clicking on her keyboard. After about a minute she said, "OK, here's your new password; write it down." She reeled off a string of letters and numbers. "Change it if you want, once you're back on line. And change the passwords on any other on-line accounts, just as a precaution."

She asked if I had my hard drive backed up. I did, I said, and the storage device was still sitting there, under my desk. "Well," she said, "except for leaving your back-up device where it could be lost along with your computer, you did the right thing."

The management of my condo building, seeking to forestall any anxiety among the residents, said that they would have someone in the lobby twenty-four-seven for the next several days. Morrie said he was willing to send security personnel wherever I wanted them, but I told him that it didn't look like it would be necessary.

My last call was to Elsie Follen. Bruno was hanging in there, she said. The x-rays showed some broken ribs, as she had suspected, and some internal damage. It looked as though someone had kicked him, she said, and hard. But his breathing had improved and the bleeding had stopped. It was still touch and go, but he had made it this far and every minute he hung on was a step toward his recovery. Let me know if there are any changes, I said. She assured me that she would. They had a cot in one of their back rooms, she said, and she was going to stay there overnight to keep an eye on him. She would call me tomorrow morning with an update. I thanked her profusely and we hung up. All this for a dumb cat, I thought. Why couldn't he just crawl under a bed? Did he have to be a hero?

A minute later my cell phone rang. It was my golfing buddy, Ted Crawford, saying he needed a fourth for a nine-thirty tee-off time Saturday morning. Was I interested? Ellis wasn't due back in town until late afternoon, and I needed a break. "Sure," I said. "Who else is playing?"

"What's the matter?" he asked. "You sound like you've been crying."

"Just a frog in my throat," I said, and cleared my throat a couple of times hoping to confirm my diagnosis. Dumb cat.

"Same guys as last time," he said. "Hey, remember our conversation about Steve Randall running for mayor, and you saying Harvey wouldn't get mixed up in politics?"

"Yes," I answered warily, certain that something was coming.

"Well, Randall announced his candidacy today, and guess who his finance director is."

"Uh, Harvey?"

"Bingo!" he said.

32

I was, I confess, stunned by Ted's news. Harvey Anderson's agreement to serve as the bag man in the campaign for mayor of an ex-criminal defense lawyer-turned-prosecutor seemed wholly out of character. Harvey was a natural-born snob. I very much doubted that he and Steven Randall were school chums or old fishing buddies or that they had any past relationship that might blossom into a political alliance. There was, of course, the chance that Randall might win, and if he did then Harvey would be sitting pretty when it came to any favors to be dispensed by the mayor's office. The city was involved in a variety of projects, some involving big money, all needing lawyering, and there undoubtedly would be more to come. Pretty crass, but so it goes. On the other hand, if Randall lost and the incumbent was re-elected, then Harvey – and his firm – would be on the outside looking in when the goodies were passed out.

And if this was part of a business development strategy by his firm, why pick Harvey for the job? There would have been plenty of other choices among his many partners. Why a trusts and estates lawyer with no political background? He did have access to old money, but would old money be likely to back a guy like Randall? I could only conclude that Harvey had wanted the job, and a theory as to why was beginning to take shape in my mind.

Saturday turned out to be one of those transition days between summer and fall. It was overcast with a cool north breeze. My cell phone rang as I was driving to the country club. It was Elsie. She reported that Bruno seemed to be better. His vital signs were OK and she had removed the IV. She thought he was going to make it, although he would need surgery to repair some of the internal damage. That was a relief.

My foursome was attired in sweaters and fleece vests and we stood around blowing on our hands before teeing off. It wasn't unpleasant, but it wasn't shirtsleeve weather either. I couldn't seem to keep my mind on my game, and I was scattering the ball all over the place. I finally settled down on the back nine and hit some decent shots, but the outing cost Ted and me a few bucks, mostly because of my play. To make it up to him, I offered to buy lunch. The other two guys had to head home.

We sat in the club's grill room, at the same table we had occupied two weeks earlier. Only three other tables were occupied, probably because of the weather. We ordered coffee, not beer, to remove the chill from our morning on the links, and I asked Ted for his take on Harvey's involvement with Randall. He confirmed my thinking.

"There's something weird going on there," he said. "Either Harvey has a reason for cozying up to Randall, or vice versa. I'm inclined to the former. There's the legal business to be done for the city if Randall wins. But still…"

"Remember when we saw him here last time?" I asked. "He was with that young lawyer from the prosecutor's office, the chief investigator assigned to Susannah Townsend's murder, and that criminal lawyer from his firm. I asked Tommy Glynn about it, and he thought the prosecutor's office might have been getting some outside advice on how to handle the Bullard case."

Ted thought. "So maybe Harvey put that meeting together? At Randall's request?" he speculated.

"Could be," I mused. Or, I thought to myself, maybe Harvey wanted to do whatever he could to help nail Bullard, and the meeting was his idea. I made a mental note to ask Ray Hammond what he knew about this.

Ellis arrived at my place about four o'clock, having foregone a stop at her house. I had spent half the day on Friday cleaning up my study so that she wouldn't be shocked by its condition. I needed to bring both her and Morrie up to date, and rather than go through it twice I called the Townsend residence to see when Morrie might be available for a meeting. He asked if we could be at his place about five-thirty, and I said we could. We drove out to his home.

We sat down in Morrie's study, a gracious room with walnut paneling, a marble fireplace, thick oriental rugs over a parquet floor and comfortable chairs. It was unsettling to walk down the hallway where I had found Susannah's body. I wondered how the family was able to live in the house with their memories of that terrible day. Morrie offered drinks. I asked for a light bourbon and water and Ellis took a glass of white wine. As if reading my mind, while he was making our drinks Morrie announced that he was putting the house on the market. He didn't need such a big place now that the children were away, or soon would be, and there were too many memories of Susannah imbedded in the home.

When we were settled, I told them about my meeting with the judge and the terms of his order, my subsequent conversation with Hammond and what I had learned from Ted Crawford about Harvey Anderson's political activities. Morrie was pleased with the outcome of my meeting with the judge, and both he and Ellis were surprised by the news about Harvey. I didn't go into my theory as to why he might have gotten involved in Randall's campaign; there was more I wanted to know. There wasn't much more to report. I told Morrie that I would keep him informed, but that matters were now pretty much in the hands of Ray Hammond.

After leaving Morrie's, Ellis and I had a late dinner at Gino's and went back to my condo. Having not seen each other for two days, we spent no further time talking. We took a shower together, toweled each other off and got straight into bed. She was warm, pliant and uninhibited and our love-making was, if possible, even better than before.

Sunday morning we drove to Ellis' house. It had not been disturbed. She packed up a suitcase and watered her plants, and we drove back to my place, stopping for groceries along the way. Drawing on my extensive gastronomic skills, I made grilled cheese sandwiches and tomato soup for lunch. We spent the rest of the day reading the papers and talking. Elsie called in the afternoon. She had dropped by her clinic to check on Bruno. He was doing OK. She was going to do the surgery tomorrow, she said. If he got through that, then she was optimistic about his full recovery.

On Monday morning, Ellis went back to work at the bank, her vacation over, such as it was. I went to my office. Having discharged the task assigned to me by Judge Callahan's order, I needed to report to him that I had done so. I called his chambers. He was starting a new trial, but had left instructions with his secretary to work me into his schedule at the first available opportunity. We agreed that I would be there at five-thirty that afternoon. I also wanted to talk further with John Martin and made an appointment to see him right after lunch. In the meantime, I caught up on my e-mails and correspondence and made some progress on the other work on my desk.

I met Martin at his office. After the preliminaries, I asked how he had found Ann Conway.

"We didn't find her," he said, "she found us. When her predecessor retired, we were about to advertise for a replacement when I got a call from Conway. She had heard about the job opening and asked if she could apply. I said sure, and she sent me her resume. It looked pretty good, and her salary requirements were reasonable."

"Did you do a background check?" I asked.

"Yes, certainly," he said. "We always do for director-level personnel. She got a clean bill of health and her references checked out."

"Was the background check done in-house?"

"No," he said, "not in this case. I happened to be talking with Harvey Anderson about the process and he offered to have his firm do it. His people were good at that sort of thing, he said, and he wouldn't charge us for the service. A couple of days later he called me with a report."

"Think back to that conversation," I said. "Do you recall, exactly, how the subject came up?"

"Let's see," he mused. "I remember that we were at one of our fundraising events in the lobby of the theater. A wine and cheese thing. I was talking with a grants officer from one of our supporting foundations and Harvey came over. We all talked for a couple of minutes and then, after the grants officer moved on, Harvey asked me how the search was going. I told him we had an interesting applicant. That was when he made the offer."

"So he initiated the conversation, not you."

"Yes, I guess that's right," John agreed. "Is that important?"

"It might be," I allowed. But I saw no reason to divulge what I had discovered about Conway's past, at least not now. Then another question occurred to me.

"Have you talked with Harvey recently?" He thought about that.

"The last time I spoke with Harvey was the day you and Ellis finished your interviews with the staff. When was that? Two weeks ago? You talked with me here in my office, and you asked me about Ann Conway's termination. I wasn't sure what I could say about either Susannah's involvement or the reasons for Ann's discharge. I wanted to talk with Morris about Susannah, but he wasn't available. I then called Harvey to get his advice on our obligations under Ann's severance agreement. I told him what you and Ellis were looking for and he said that the confidentiality provision in the agreement barred me from answering your questions. I then reported to you and Ellis that I couldn't say anything further until I had talked to Morris. Then, when I was able to reach Morris, he said I should use my own judgment as to what to say to you about Susannah. So, when you and I talked about it a day or two later, I told you that I couldn't tell you anything more."

So, two weeks ago, Harvey had learned "what I was up to," as he had put it in our conversation in the country club lounge. He knew that I was getting help from Ellis, he knew that we were interviewing the symphony staff, and he knew that we were interested in the circumstances of Ann Conway's termination. And the day Conway agreed to talk with us, she was dead.

33

My second meeting with Judge Callahan was short and to the point. I reported that I had complied with the terms of his order, and he produced an affidavit that I was to sign stating that fact. His secretary came in, I signed the affidavit, and she notarized it. The affidavit also would be sealed, the judge said, and filed as part of the record in the Bullard case. He asked if I was comfortable with the steps we had taken, and I said that I was. He thanked me for my cooperation with the court, I submitted to another bone-crushing handshake, and was on my way.

Driving home, I had a call from Ray Hammond. He didn't want to talk on the phone, he said, but there had been a development. Could we meet at my office in twenty minutes? I agreed, told him that I also had some news for him, and called Ellis to tell her I would be delayed getting home. She told me that Elsie had called. Bruno's surgery had gone as well as could be expected, and she was confident that he was going to recover.

I was the first to arrive at Carrolton Associates. A guard from the security service I had hired to watch the office was sitting in our reception area, reading a detective novel. I tapped on the glass, pointed to my name on the door and held up my ID. He let me in and I introduced myself. When Ray Hammond showed up a few minutes later, the guard said, "Hi, Ray, how you doing?"

"I'm good, Gil. You OK?"

"Yeah," the guard said. "I'm fine. Being retired is a blast. I get to sit around all night in empty reception rooms waiting for bad guys to show up. At least it's more fun than watching reality shows on TV. Pays better, too."

Ray and I walked down the hall and sat in my office. He asked me how it had gone with Judge Callahan, and I affirmed that it had gone well, as expected.

"Good," he said. Then, "Well, listen to this. I'm at the station this afternoon, doing some paperwork, and I have to go to the john. I'm in there, washing my hands, when in walks a young cop that I barely know, new to the force. His name's Elliot Lamey. I'm looking at him in the mirror and I see his face is all scratched up...really bad cuts. His hands, too. Jeez, I say, what happened to you? Aw, he says, I was doing some yard work over the weekend and fell into a rosebush. Scratched the hell out of me. Too bad! I say. Thanks, he says. I'll live.

"So," Ray continued, "I didn't think anything more about it for an hour or two, but then I found myself wondering how he got so beat up by a rosebush. On a hunch, I guess, I looked up his address. Turns out he lives in that high-rise on the river, over by the university. It's surrounded by asphalt. He has no yard and no rosebush, either. He didn't say it was his yard he was working in, but he didn't say it wasn't. Maybe he was helping out his folks, or a girlfriend, but now I'm thinking maybe those are cat scratches and maybe it's your cat that did it. In any case, just to clear things up, I send an e-mail to the DNA guys asking them to compare what we got from your cat to the DNA we have on file for Lamey. I should hear back on that in a day or two.

"But it's a pretty ugly thing, thinking that a cop might have broken into your place. And worse, if it was him, who might have asked him to do it? There's no reason to think that Lamey had any interest in your computer. If he did the break-in, he had to have been working for someone else...maybe someone involved in the Townsend case? What else on your computer would be of interest to anyone other than a tax geek? But I can't figure out how anyone in your cast of characters might be connected to Lamey."

I thought I could. I asked, "You know that Randall is running for mayor?' He did. "Did you see who is finance chairman is?" He had not. I told him. "The guy who had the affair with Conway?" he asked. I nodded. "Oh, shit!" he said. We were both quiet for a minute or so while he considered the implications of this news.

"Let me ask you another question," I said. "I was at the country club the day you met for lunch with Anderson, Chris Goodman and Jason Plaskett. I assume that was about the Bullard case?"

"Yeah, it was," he said. "I thought I saw you there."

"Who set that meeting up?"

He thought about it. "I guess I'm not sure," he responded. "Plaskett called me and said that Goodman had offered to help with his preparation of the Bullard case. Goodman has a reputation around town as a good criminal lawyer and Plaskett wanted to see what he had to say. He wanted me there and I said, sure, when? He said that Goodman was going to be playing golf at the country club on Saturday and we were going to meet there for lunch after his round, about twelve-thirty. It's not often a black guy gets invited to lunch at the country club, so I said OK. When I got there, Plaskett and Goodman were sitting with Anderson, and I joined them. I thought it was odd that Anderson was there, but I assumed that he and Goodman had been playing golf together. He didn't say much during the meeting. I guess it could have been his idea. I didn't have the impression that Plaskett had approached Goodman."

"Well," I said, "it's at least possible, if not probable, that the meeting was Anderson's idea, and that he was doing what he could to help nail Bullard. And consider this," I said, and went on to tell him what I had learned that afternoon in my conversation with John Martin.

"Boy," he said. "This just gets better and better. But I still don't see why Anderson is involved in all this."

I had spent a lot of time thinking about how Harvey could have been stealing from the symphony, and why, and I now had a theory. I rolled it out for Ray. He thought about it, asked a few questions, and ultimately agreed that I might be right.

I arrived home about seven-thirty and Ellis had dinner almost ready. She actually had on an apron. I gave her a kiss and said, "Don't look now, honeybun, but I think we've settled down."

She laughed, and turned back to her cooking. But I thought I saw a wistful look cross her face.

34

Ray Hammond called me the next morning, about ten o'clock. The DNA test results were in. It was Elliot Lamey who broke into my home and kicked my cat. I am not a violent man but if, at that moment, Lamey had been standing in front of me and I had my hands on an appropriate implement, I am certain that I would have done my best to cause him grievous bodily harm.

"I've been thinking about how to handle this," Ray said. "I want to get the chief involved. He needs to know, and I want to protect my backside. I don't know the chief all that well, but he and Tommy are old friends and I think we should talk with him about our approach. I don't want to waltz in there and start pushing the wrong buttons."

At two o'clock that afternoon, Ray, Tommy and I were seated in my office. "OK," I said to Tommy once we were settled. "Here's where we are. I've had my meeting with Judge Callahan, like we discussed. As a result of that meeting, I've told Ray about Susannah Townsend's request for my help and my subsequent investigation. He now knows everything I know. He and I are both subject to an order from the judge maintaining the confidentiality of that information. When and how it ultimately may be disclosed will be up to Callahan. But another situation has come up, and here's where we need your help." And I went on to tell him about the attempt to hack into my office computer system, the break-in at my condo, and the identification of a police officer as the person who did the job. Tommy looked askance.

"It gets worse," I continued. "There's no reason to think that Lamey was acting on his own. He would have done the break-in only if someone had asked him to do it. Do you know Harvey Anderson?"

"No," he said, "but I've heard you mention his name."

"He's a partner in a big downtown law firm and one of his clients is the symphony. He was having an affair with the symphony's development director, a woman named Ann Conway. His wife found out about it and told Susannah Townsend that Conway was involved in an improper relationship that affected the symphony. Susannah got her fired. Then Susannah comes to me for help on a symphony matter. Then Susannah is killed. Steve Randall charges Albert Bullard with Susannah's murder. Harvey Anderson goes out of his way to help Randall with the prosecution. I begin an investigation into Susannah's concerns and Ann Conway's name pops up as a person of interest in that matter. She agrees, reluctantly, to talk with me, and then she's killed. Then, just a few days ago, Randall announces that he's running for mayor, and Harvey is his campaign finance director."

I paused, and then continued. "I think that Randall got Lamey to do the break-in. Maybe it was part of a quid pro quo for Harvey's agreement to support his campaign. The only thing taken was my computer. Harvey called me last week probing for information on my investigation, which I didn't give him, and he suggested that I drop the matter. I think he asked Randall to get someone to steal my computer. He's trying to find out what I know about Susannah's problem, and I think that's because he's part of that problem. But here's where we bump up against Judge Callahan's order. I can't disclose what that involves."

Tommy spent a few moments digesting this. "So you think the county prosecutor – who is running for mayor – got a cop to do an illegal break-in and steal your computer as a favor to a big shot lawyer? And that this lawyer may be a killer?"

I nodded. "That's it in a nutshell."

"Christ!" he exclaimed. "Tell me you're kidding."

"I wish we were," Ray said. "We know there's a lot that doesn't make sense, at least not yet. But you can see how sensitive this is. And that's where you come in. Are you still in touch with Chief Matthews?"

"Yeah," Tommy said. "We're close. Always have been, ever since we were beat cops together. He was my mentor. He and his wife are my kids' godparents. He's a fine guy. I hope you don't think he has any involvement in this."

"No, not at all," Ray assured him. "Just the opposite. From everything I know about the chief, he wouldn't tolerate anything like this. I want to put him in the loop and get his agreement on what happens next."

"Mmm," Tommy said. He thought a moment. "And you want me to run interference."

"Right," Ray said. "We've got several issues here, and at the top of my list is how to deal with a dirty cop, but I don't think he's the place to start in unraveling this mess. If we take Lamey down, the boys up the chain are going to see what's coming. But he's going to get nailed at some point and we may wind up implicating Steve Randall. I don't want the chief to be surprised when that happens. Once we start to pull on the strings, this could get ugly fast. The chief's got to know what's coming and when."

"OK," Tommy said. "Let me digest this." We sat quietly for a minute or two while he worked it over in his mind. "Here's the sticky part," he said. "The only hard evidence you have is Lamey's DNA. That ties him to the break-in at Alex's place, but the rest of it – Anderson's involvement, Randall's involvement – is supposition, right?"

"Right," I said.

"And you can't tell me – or the chief – what's behind all this...why Anderson and Randall might be involved in a criminal conspiracy?"

"Right again. But Ray and I are agreed on a theory."

"Well," Tommy said, "theory or not, that's going to be a difficult conversation."

"Does this help?" I asked, and gave him a copy of the letter to Ray from Judge Callahan in which the judge had described how Ray was to use the confidential information I had given him. Tommy read it.

"Yeah," he said, "it does, I think." He thought a moment more. "Well," he continued, "I agree that you need to get in front of the chief. I'll go with you. You give him the Lamey piece of this, how you came to have the letter from Callahan, and a copy of the letter. How much you tell him about Randall is up to you, but my recommendation is that you give him everything you've got, even if it's only guesswork. If there's any chance that Randall is going down over this, the sooner Matthews knows, the better."

"OK," I said, "good. But a lot of people will see us if we go parading into police headquarters and down the hall to the chief's office. I think we should see if he would come here."

"All right," Tommy said. "I'll call him right now."

Chief Mark Matthews arrived at my offices forty-five minutes later. I had told our receptionist that he was expected, and she ushered him straight into our meeting. He was in plain clothes, of medium height with a solid build, thick black hair and dark eyes. He looked very fit. Tommy introduced me and told Matthews about our business relationship. He said hello to Ray, and we sat down. Ray and I then went through the whole story as we had described it to Tommy, our belief that Harvey Anderson and Steve Randall were involved, and the circumstances of the letter to Ray from Judge Callahan. Matthews didn't ask any questions until we had finished. He then turned to Tommy and said,

"What do you think about all this?"

"It's not pretty, Mark," Tommy said, "but there's no real doubt about Lamey's involvement in the break-in at Alex's place. I know Alex pretty well and I trust his judgment and his instincts. He and Ray are agreed on a theory that links all of this together and Ray has the information protected by Judge Callahan's order. I don't know what that is, but we both know Ray is a good cop, so if he thinks that information implicates this Anderson guy, or Randall, then it does, as far as I'm concerned."

The chief turned to Hammond. "Ray," he said, "is that right? Do you think these guys are involved?"

"Yes, Chief, I do." Ray said. "I'd have to say I have enough to warrant a closer look at both of them."

Chief Matthews thought for a couple of moments. "OK," he said. "Stay on it. But keep me advised."

After Tommy and the chief left my office, Ray and I sat back down and talked about what to do next. It wasn't going to be easy to come up with any evidence directly implicating Harvey or Steve Randall. We had no facts to support my theory and, in Ray's opinion, nothing sufficient to support a request for a search warrant.

There was even less that tied Harvey to the deaths of Susannah or Ann Conway, and we couldn't get to Randall without yanking on Lamey's chain. After kicking all of this around for a few minutes and getting nowhere, I came up with an idea. I had promised Harvey that, when my investigation into Susannah's problem was concluded, I would give him a report. I could call him and tell him that I was ready to hand over what I had.

When I got to that meeting, I would be wearing a wire.

35

"You're not going in there alone," Ellis said when I described my plan to her that evening. "This guy's already killed two people! If you're going to confront him with anything, I'm going to be there."

"I'll be fine," I said. "The meeting will be in his law office. There'll be a lot of people around. Ray Hammond will be in the lobby of the building, just an elevator ride away, listening to everything. He can be there in two minutes. If Harvey gets really nasty, I can walk out of the room at any time." All this I believed, but it was at least possible that the meeting would result in a dust-up of some kind and I didn't want to put Ellis in any danger. She turned my argument around on me.

"OK," she said. "If it's going to be so easy, then there's no reason I shouldn't be there. And if there are two people for him to deal with, then there's less risk of anything happening. It'd be better all around," she concluded, the conversation at an end, in her opinion.

I thought about it. She had a point about the safety-in-numbers argument, and I really didn't expect that the meeting would result in violence.

"All right," I said, "if it's OK with Ray."

"Leave Ray to me," she said.

The next morning, I called Ray from my office. He agreed that Ellis could join the meeting, so it would not be necessary to unleash her on him. In our meeting the day before, he and I had agreed that there was one question raised by my plan that we needed to resolve. My next call was to Priscilla Freitag.

"I have a legal research project for you," I said. "Short timetable. Can you get on this right away?"

"Sure can," she said. "What's the question?"

"Let me give you a hypothetical," I said. "A private citizen agrees to wear a wire to a meeting with a suspect in a criminal investigation. The wire feed goes to the cops. In that meeting, the suspect admits his involvement in the crime. No *Miranda* warning, no warrant, no due process. The question is, can the admission be used against the suspect?"

"You're not going to do something stupid, are you?" she asked.

"I hope not," I said, "but I need to know the answer to the question."

"Yeah," she said, "I'm pretty sure it can. But let me double check. I'll send you some authority. Give me thirty minutes." I thanked her and hung up. About fifteen minutes later I received an e-mail with four attached articles discussing the question and citations to Supreme Court cases that confirmed Priscilla's opinion. This girl had a future in the law business, I thought. I forwarded her e-mail to Ray.

Thus armed, I called Harvey. I told him that I was ready to report my findings on the investigation into Susannah's problem and would like to meet with him for that purpose. I said that Ellis Kirkland had been assisting in the investigation – which he already knew from John Martin – and that she also would attend our meeting. He seemed surprised by my call.

"Last time we talked," he said, "I was under the impression that you were going to pull the plug on this. What's there to report?"

"I've come up with some information that might be of interest to the symphony trustees," I said, "and I still think you're in the best position assess its significance and convey it to them. That was what you wanted, wasn't it?"

"Well," he conceded, "yes, it was. OK. I can see you here tomorrow at ten-thirty. That all right with you?" I said it was, and we hung up.

Ray Hammond and a police department technician showed up at my condo at eight-thirty the next morning. I had expected that they would be lugging a case of electronic equipment and I would be rigged up with a microphone, antenna and duct tape. It turned out that all the tech had to do was insert a black plastic chip, about half the size of a matchbook, into a seam in my suit coat. He then ran a series of checks and announced that I was good to go. The tech explained that the chip contained a SIM card, which he had already programmed and activated, and a transmitter. It would pick up any sounds within about thirty-five feet. There was no distance limitation on the transmission; it worked like a cell phone. The built-in battery would last about six hours. There would be an unmarked police van parked on the street outside Harvey's building with recording equipment. Ray would be able to monitor what was going on through an ear piece.

They left, and Ellis and I had about an hour to kill before heading to Harvey's office. Knowing that we were wired imposed a certain restraint on our conversation. After a few minutes of saying almost nothing at all, I walked over to where she was standing and put my arms around her, then slid my hands down over her trim rear end and pulled her into me. She suppressed a giggle and squirmed but couldn't tell me to cut it out. I gave her a big sloppy kiss. She laughed out loud and finally twisted away from me, grinning from ear to ear. Just you wait! she mouthed at me.

I couldn't spot the police van on the street, but when we arrived at Harvey's building we saw Ray Hammond sitting in one of the lobby chairs, reading a newspaper. As I passed behind him I could see a small earpiece behind his right ear. If I hadn't been looking for it, I wouldn't have noticed. We got on the elevator and rode up to the eleventh floor. The building housing Harvey's firm was a modern glass and steel structure, but the décor in his reception area was old school – walnut paneling, oriental carpets, and a bust of the firm's founder in a wall niche opposite the elevators. We announced ourselves to the receptionist, but were a few minutes early, so we sat down. I pulled out my cell phone and called Ray. He answered on the first ring.

"I hear you just fine," he said. "Relax." I hung up.

A few minutes later Harvey Anderson walked into the lobby and greeted us. "Come on in," he said, and led us down a long hallway. I noted that his private office was not on the corner of the building; Harvey hadn't yet achieved that milestone. He installed himself behind his impressive desk and Ellis and I took the two side chairs opposite. The chairs seemed low, probably by design, so that Harvey would have the height advantage over whomever he was dealing with. The room wasn't large and he had too much furniture in it. Harvey's tastes in art apparently ran to the English Old Masters. There were two reproductions on the walls in ornate frames. Constable, I thought. His view was to the north; I could see my condo building a few blocks away.

"Well," he said, "what have you got for me?" His desk was cluttered with files and books. He cleared a small area in front of his chair and prepared to take notes on a legal pad.

Conscious that we were making a record, I began. I hoped that whatever digital wizardry I was hooked up to was working. "Harvey," I said, "as you know I was hired by Susannah Townsend to look into her concerns regarding a possible embezzlement from the symphony. You suggested to her that she engage me for that purpose, and she did. After her death, Morris Townsend asked me to continue with that assignment, and I have since been representing him.

"My first step was to talk with Ellis. Susannah told me that she had talked with her about the embezzlement and I thought that, as the symphony's treasurer, she was the logical place to start." Harvey looked at Ellis, and looked back at me.

"Subsequently," I said, "Ellis and I interviewed each of the symphony's staff members, treating Susannah's information as a matter governed by its whistleblower policy. Those interviews revealed nothing that seemed relevant to an embezzlement except that the symphony's development director, Ann Conway, had been let go a few months ago. We were told that she was having an affair with someone associated with the symphony, and that she also might have been involved in some improper activities related to her job." Harvey seemed to stiffen slightly. "We made an appointment to talk with her, but shortly thereafter she was killed in a fall from her apartment in upstate New York."

"Yes," Harvey said. "I heard about that." He hadn't taken any notes so far.

"Also," I went on, "I found a note in Susannah's symphony files referring to something called the XYZ Trust. As it happens, Ellis' bank has a relationship with the trust, and I was able to talk with Gordon Parker about it." Harvey was now glaring at me.

"Parker was reluctant to talk with us, but we agreed that we would keep what he said confidential. He described the purpose of the trust and also said that Susannah had raised a question with him about the amount of its first distribution to the symphony. He assured her that, according to his records, the distribution had been made correctly. He also said that you are the trustee. I was impressed. It must be gratifying to have the confidence of people like the Tichner family."

"Parker has a big mouth," Harvey said, ignoring my compliment. "And you, Ellis – aren't you supposed to be the bank's compliance officer? Why did you let him talk with Alex?"

"It wasn't a compliance issue, Harvey," Ellis said. "I advised Gordon that he should use his own judgment as to what was in the best interests of the trust. What's the problem? There hasn't been a leak about the trust's activities."

Harvey put down his pen, leaned back in his chair, crossed his arms over his chest and said, "Go on."

This is where our discussion would become unpleasant. I hoped that we were still plugged into Ray Hammond.

36

I saw no reason to dance around. "OK," I said. "Here's what I think. Let me know if I get off track.

"First, it seems obvious that Susannah wasn't satisfied with Parker's answer to her question about the trust distribution. She probably talked with the chairpersons of the other trust beneficiaries about the size of their distributions and compared those amounts to the estimates Parker had given them and what the symphony had received. For whatever reason, I think she came to the conclusion that the amount deposited in the symphony's account at the bank was less than what it should have been. A lot less. Conway was the only other person at the symphony who knew about the trust, so Susannah was suspicious that she might be involved in whatever had gone wrong.

"Then she gets a tip through her grapevine about Conway's affair, and also hears that someone – she isn't told who – is stealing from the symphony. Rightly or wrongly, she puts two and two together and concludes that Conway is a thief. But she has no proof, and isn't even sure what's happened. In any event, she had lost confidence in Conway as a development officer, and it was an easy step to the conclusion that she had to go. So she gets John Martin to fire her. Eventually she tells Ellis about her concerns, and talks to you, and that's where I come in."

I paused and took a breath. Ellis was rigid in her chair. Harvey hadn't moved a muscle.

"Unfortunately, Harvey," I said, "there's a lot here that points to you. I know that you were instrumental in getting Conway her job.

I'm guessing that you knew she had a criminal background and figured she was corruptible. I also know it was you that she was having the affair with. Let's assume for the moment that the two of you conspired to steal from the symphony. How would you do that? And why? Let's start with how.

"My guess is that some part of the XYZ Trust distribution was diverted to Conway and then to you. It would have to be done in a way that balanced the trust's account at the bank. You're the trustee and you authorized the beneficiary distributions. Maybe you shorted the amount to be distributed to the symphony's agency account by the intra-bank transfer and wrote checks to the symphony for the difference. From the bank's perspective, both payments go through the account, so the account balances. You then give the checks to Conway. She forges the symphony's endorsement on the checks and deposits them in phony accounts that she sets up in its name. You and she then divide up the pot. And you're set up to do the same thing again for the next two distributions. So, by December, when it's all over, we could be talking about a lot of money, maybe two or three million dollars, maybe more. The trust shuts down, and no one has any reason to ask any questions."

Harvey still hadn't moved, but his face was flushed and I thought his hands were trembling. That might be the reaction of an innocent man, falsely accused, as well as a guilty one. But I was into it now, so I went on.

"But what's your motive? You're a lawyer with a big reputation and a partner in a big firm. You probably make a lot of money. But how much is enough? I don't know that much about your lifestyle, but maybe you've got some expensive bad habits. Ann Conway, for example. Maybe you look around at what your partners are making as deal lawyers or big-time litigators and decide that trust and estates work is undervalued. You deserve more. Whatever the reason, there's the question why you would go for a home run…steal a couple of million dollars, if that's the right number, rather than some less noticeable amount. Again, I don't know, but maybe you've been stealing small but increasing amounts from several of your trust accounts for a long time, covering up when necessary by replacing what you've taken with funds from another account, and it finally caught up with you. Or maybe Conway was blackmailing you, threatening to tell your wife about your affair. Or all of the above."

Harvey was now glaring at me. He sat up straight in his chair and pointed his finger at me. "You've got a lot of nerve," he said, "coming in here and accusing me. This is outrageous. Do you have any proof of anything? Why should I even be talking to you?"

"You're right," I said. "I don't have any proof. But there's more circumstantial evidence that points in your direction. Do you know a cop named Elliot Lamey?"

My question seemed to catch him by surprise. "No," he said. But he didn't ask what Lamey had to do with him. I didn't believe him.

"If it's proof you want," I said, "I can suggest to the Tichner family that they ask for a full accounting of your actions as trustee. Bring in a forensic auditor. Or ask Gordon Parker to do so. Or talk to the symphony board. If I'm right, there's got to be a paper trail somewhere. If nothing turns up, I'll apologize."

That shook him, but he recovered and retaliated. "You'd do more than apologize," he said. "I'd sue you for defamation before the sun went down." I shrugged.

"I wouldn't have to defame you. I don't think it would take much to get an inquiry going."

I had expected that, by the time we had come this far, Harvey would have cracked and said something that would incriminate him. But he hadn't. He was rattled but still denying everything. I played my next card.

"Here's another question, Harvey," I said. "Who killed Susannah? And Ann Conway?"

"You bastard!" he said. "Are you accusing me of murder?"

"Again, Harvey, there's circumstantial evidence. You seem very interested in pinning Susannah's murder on Albert Bullard. You've cozied up to Steve Randall. You brought in some firepower from your firm to help him prepare his case. Maybe we're going to find that some of the XYZ money has found its way to his campaign. And there's motive. If Susannah had figured out what you were up to, you'd have had a good reason to silence her. Just before Ann Conway died, you found out that Ellis and I were going to talk with her. Maybe you knew, or feared, that she would cave in and implicate you. Maybe all that cash from the trust was sitting around, within reach, and you decided there was no reason to split it with her. Let me ask you this: can you account for your whereabouts at the time each of them was killed?"

With that last question, something changed in Harvey. His shoulders slumped and his face took on a wholly different aspect – stoic, hardened, unfeeling. He opened his top desk drawer and reached inside. When he pulled his hand back out, he was holding a gun.

37

"All right," Harvey said. "That's enough. Here's what we're going to do. We're going to stand up and walk out of here. I'll be right behind you. You will walk to the elevators and we'll get on. Neither of you will say or do anything that calls attention to us, or Ellis gets shot. Her first, then you. Let's go." He stood up and waved us toward the door with the gun.

I was dumbfounded. I knew that I was pushing Harvey pretty hard but I had not anticipated that he would snap. Obviously, he had no alibi, and that fact had triggered his reaction to my last question. My next thought was about Ray Hammond. Harvey's threat to shoot us would have put him in motion. But if Ray was now jumping on an elevator, there was the chance that we would pass him on the way up while we were going down. Neither of us had anticipated this situation. What have I gotten us into, I wondered.

We walked to the elevator lobby and Harvey pushed the down button. He had his hand in his suit coat pocket, with the gun. We had to wait a minute for an elevator to arrive. I found myself hoping that, when the doors opened, Ray would be standing inside with the muzzle of his gun pointed right between Harvey's eyes. But then I realized that, for all my baiting of Harvey, he hadn't confessed to anything. He had committed a new crime by abducting Ellis and me at gunpoint, but he had said nothing incriminating about the theft or the murders. If we were going to achieve that objective, we needed more time. But at what cost?

The doors opened and the elevator was empty. Harvey nodded to us to get in first, and he followed, moving around behind us.

"Push P-2," he said.

"The parking garage?" I asked, for Ray's benefit.

"Just push it," Harvey said. I did. The elevator stopped twice, taking on more passengers. No one said anything. They got off at the ground floor, and we continued on to the garage level. I didn't think there would have been sufficient time for Ray to have arrived there ahead of us. When the doors opened, no one else was in sight.

"Over there," Harvey said, gesturing toward a white sedan. I realized that it was the same car I had seen parked in Susannah's driveway when I arrived at her house on the afternoon she was killed. "The white sedan?" I said, again for Ray's benefit, wondering if the wire transmission was reaching through the layers of concrete in the basement garage. Harvey gave me a push. "Move," he said. "Get in the front seat. You drive. I'll be behind you. You'll do what I say."

I got in behind the steering wheel and Ellis sat in the passenger seat. Harvey now had the gun out of his pocket and kept it pointed at us as he got in the back seat, behind Ellis. I started the car. "Go out the east exit," Harvey said, "and turn north. The pass card is under the visor. Use it."

"All right," I said, leaving the garage. "I'm turning north. Where are we going?"

"Shut up," Harvey said. "Just drive." I was dropping all the bread crumbs I could, but I had no idea if Ray knew where we were.

There wasn't much traffic given the late morning hour, and we moved steadily north, out of the downtown business district and into the older residential area on the north side. We were on the main road leading out of town. Ellis seemed surprisingly calm, given the gun at her back. I was kicking myself for letting her talk me into attending the meeting with Harvey. I kept checking the rear view mirror to see if I could spot the police van or anyone else following us. Nothing.

"Harvey," I said, finally, "this isn't going to work. A lot of people know that Ellis and I are looking into a theft from the symphony.

You're in this way too deep. If anything happens to us, you're going to get a lot of attention from the police."

"Let me worry about that," he said.

"No, Harvey," I said. "Think about it. You're better off giving yourself up."

"Yeah, right," he said. "I go to the police and tell them that I killed Suzannah Townsend and stole two million dollars from a client, and they tell me not to do it again and let me go." He laughed. "No," he said, "I've got a better plan. With you two out of the way, I can buy the time I need. I have some unfinished business with the XYZ Trust."

Well, I thought, for whatever it's worth, at least we have him on record with a confession.

We kept moving north, out of the city and into the suburbs, passing within a few blocks of Susannah's home, and kept going. We had been driving for almost an hour and were out into the countryside when Harvey said, "Take the next left, up there."

"Where?" I said, looking around as if confused. "County Road 241?"

"Yes, damn it," he said. "Do you see anywhere else to go?"

I turned. There were corn fields on both sides of the road. The corn had been harvested and the stubble was all that remained. Still no sign that the police were following us. After going about three miles we came to a dirt road running north.

"Turn here," Harvey said. There was no sign marking the road and I had run out of strategies for describing our position to the police, if they were still tracking our movements. After a mile or so the corn fields ended and we drove into a wooded area. The dirt road turned into a two-track. A few hundred yards farther on, we came to an opening in the trees maybe ten acres in size. The land had been used for gravel extraction at one time, but no longer. At the far end was an abandoned pit. The road went up a small rise on the east side of the cleared area and ended. There was a large pile of dirt on the south side of the pit, covered with weeds, and water standing at the bottom of the excavation.

"Stop the car," Harvey said. I did, and he stepped out, still holding the gun on us. "Get out. Leave the keys." Ellis looked at me with a question in her eyes. I had to admit to myself that this didn't look good. If Harvey shot us here and threw our bodies in the water, it was not likely they would ever be found. I contemplated jamming the car into reverse and stomping on the accelerator, but Harvey was standing just outside Ellis' window and I couldn't risk his getting off a shot at her. I nodded to Ellis that she should do as Harvey had ordered. I turned off the ignition and we both got out of the car.

"Nice and quiet here, isn't it?" Harvey said, not taking his eyes off us. "Henry Tichner started buying up farm land out here in the '50's and '60's. Wound up with over 10,000 acres. Turned out to be a great investment."

Under the circumstances, I found it difficult to appreciate Henry's foresight.

"OK," Harvey said, "over there," motioning with the gun toward the edge of the pit, about two hundred yards away. We started walking through tall grass, kicking up clouds of grasshoppers as we went.

"Why did you kill Susannah?" I asked.

"Same reason as you," he said. "She figured it out. We were standing in her kitchen, waiting for you to show up. She called me right after lunch that day and more or less ordered me to be at her house at three o'clock. When I got there, she said she had just learned that I was the trustee of the XYZ Trust. You were coming and I was to explain to you how the trust operated. She was certain there was some problem with the trust's distribution to the symphony. Then, suddenly, she looked at me and said, it had to be me; I was the thief. I don't know how she did it; it seemed to come to her in a flash. I denied it, of course, but she was insistent. It all fit together, she said. It was me. She was a smart cookie, that's for sure. Then she heard your car in the driveway and started out of the room. I couldn't let her tell you. I grabbed the knife and – well, you know the rest."

"Harvey," I said. "You're insane. Poor Susannah. She trusted you. How could you kill her in cold blood?" He didn't answer.

"And Ann Conway?" I said.

"You have it mostly right," he said. "I was there, sitting in her office in New York, when she got the call from Ellis. I'd driven all night to get there after I found out from Martin that you were asking questions about her. I kept whispering to her to say no, not to agree to meet with you. But she caved in, the stupid bitch. I sure as hell couldn't trust her to keep her mouth shut." He was silent for a moment.

"But that was actually an accident," he said. "When we got to her apartment, after work, we were still arguing about it. We started pushing and shoving at each other. She lunged at me, lost her balance, and fell over the balcony railing."

Ray Hammond had told me that Conway had been murdered, so Harvey was lying despite the absence of any reason for him to do so.

"You're a dirt bag, Harvey," Ellis said, the first words she had uttered since we left his office. "Do you enjoy killing women?" He didn't react, thankfully. He actually seemed to be thinking about her question.

"Tell me something else," I said. "Why did you send Susannah to me?"

He laughed. "That was easy," he said. "I had to give her somebody. I was afraid that, if my firm handled the investigation, they would sort out what happened. Our guys were too smart. So I gave her some ridiculous estimate of what it would cost if we did the work, told her it would take a couple of months, and suggested she talk to you. I was sure that you'd get nowhere and give up." We kept walking. "I guess I was wrong about that," he said. "My mistake. Too bad for you."

We reached the edge of the pit, and Ellis and I turned around. I had one last card to play.

"Harvey," I said, "this is hopeless. I'm wearing a wire. Everything you've told us is now in the hands of the police. Here," I said, and forced the plastic chip out of the seam in my jacket. I held it out to him. He didn't seem to understand what I was saying. He looked confused.

"That thing's a wire?" he said.

"It is," I said. "Give it up. It's over. Hand me the gun."

"Like hell I will," he said. "You're bluffing." But he seemed unsure what to do next. Just then I picked up the sound of helicopter blades somewhere off to my right, behind the dirt pile and the tall trees south of us. Harvey, preoccupied, didn't notice. With surprising suddenness, the chopper appeared from behind the pile and pulled up, just a few yards above us. I could see a police SWAT team member in full body armor sitting in the open side door, sighting down an automatic rifle. The downwash beat over us, throwing up a cloud of dust.

"Police!" a voice announced over a loudspeaker. "Drop the weapon. Put your hands on your head and take two steps backward." Harvey didn't respond. He seemed in a trance.

"I said drop it!" the voice demanded. The noise, the wind and the dust created a confused, other-worldly maelstrom around us.

"Yes," Harvey then said to Ellis, shouting to be heard. "I guess I do enjoy it. Killing women, I mean. You're next."

At this point, several things happened almost simultaneously. Harvey raised his gun, which had been vaguely aimed in my direction, toward Ellis and sighted down the barrel. I threw myself to my right, between Ellis and Harvey. There were two cracks, the first one loud and close and the second louder and farther away. I felt a searing pain in my right shoulder, and the world spun around as I tumbled down the embankment of the gravel pit, toward the water.

Harvey's head exploded.

38

"Ready about," I said.

"Aye, aye, skipper," Ellis said, and gave a smart salute.

"Hard alee," I said, and put the helm down to starboard. The bow of the small catboat swung into the wind. I uncleated the mainsheet and released the tension. The sail luffed, and Ellis and I shifted to the starboard side. Ellis helped me get the sheet back into the cleat on the centerboard trunk as the sail filled on the new tack. My right arm was not yet functioning normally. She studied the set of the sail. "A little soft on the luff," she said, and trimmed the sheet another six inches. "There," she said. "Perfect." She had learned a lot in six days. My collarbone was still healing, although the doctors had assured me that I would fully recover my strength. The exercises I was doing twice a day were helping. The boat gathered speed and heeled slightly in a fresh puff of wind. We moved up onto the rail and I pulled on the tiller to counteract the weather helm – a characteristic of catboats.

Her bank had told Ellis to take a leave of absence until she was ready to come back to work. She wanted to go to the Michigan cottage for a couple of weeks as soon as my condition permitted. I called the owner and made the arrangements. We had spent the days sailing, hiking, reading and enjoying each other's company. The weather had been perfect. Indian summer in Northern Michigan. Warm, sunny days; cool, crisp nights. It was late October, six weeks since our final encounter with Harvey Anderson on the edge of the gravel pit.

After being hit by Harvey's bullet and rolling down the embankment, I wound up in the water, unconscious. The helicopter landed.

Ray Hammond jumped out, slid down the side of the pit and lifted my head clear of the water. They got a stretcher out of the chopper and, with some difficulty, Ray and the SWAT team guy carried me up the incline through the loose stones. Ellis and I were airlifted to the university hospital, downtown, and I went straight into surgery. There was nothing to be done for Harvey. He made the trip back in a coroner's van, in a body bag.

Ellis was waiting in my private room when I got out of recovery. She remained there, sitting by my side – my good side – and holding my hand. My other arm was trussed up in a brace to keep my shoulder from moving. The bullet had broken my collar bone and caused a lot of soft tissue damage, but nothing permanent. I was lucky. Two inches to the left, the doctors said, and it wouldn't have been so easy to fix. If at all. The slug was sitting in a paper cup beside my bed, a souvenir. The contusions and abrasions I had suffered in my tumble down the embankment were only a minor annoyance.

Morrie entered the room. He had come to the hospital after getting the news from Ellis and sat in the waiting room during my surgery. Ellis had described to him what had happened.

"Thank God you're both OK," he said. "I thank you and Susannah thanks you. I now think I can put her to rest." There wasn't anything I could say in response. I was gratified that Morrie was able to find closure in what had happened. Ellis went over and kissed his check. "We'll talk more when you're better," he said. "I don't want to wear you out." And he left.

A short time later Laura burst into the room. "Alex," she said, "are you all right? What on earth happened? I had the car radio on driving home from work and they said you'd been shot." I assured her that I was OK. It was then that she noticed Ellis.

"Oh," she said. "Hi. I'm Laura."

"This is Ellis Kirkland," I said. "We're friends." Laura looked at me, and then back at Ellis, and then said, "I see. Very nice to meet you."

"It's a pleasure to meet you," Ellis said. "I've heard so many good things about you from Alex."

I didn't sense any hostility in Laura; she seemed to accept that things had changed for me, as they had for her. We talked for several minutes, during which I explained, in general terms, what had happened that day, and why, and Laura left, promising to call Becky.

A nurse came in and announced that visiting hours were over, at least for me. Ellis said she would be back first thing in the morning. I was given some pills, the nurse watched while I swallowed them, and in no time at all I was asleep.

I was released from the hospital after another thirty-six hours had elapsed with no adverse change in my condition. Ellis drove me to her house. She insisted that I stay with her until I was fully functional again. When we opened the front door, there was Bruno, as if he had been waiting for my arrival. Ellis had picked him up from the vet the previous afternoon and brought him home. He was a little stiff, like me, but otherwise seemed fine. I was glad to see him but, after briefly checking me out, he retreated to a chair in the living room and went to sleep. We could talk later, I guessed. Compare notes on our surgeries.

Ray Hammond, Chief Matthews and a deputy mayor arrived the next morning with a court stenographer. Ray had arrived in the parking garage just as Ellis, Harvey and I were pulling out in Harvey's car. He hadn't picked up my comment about the white sedan but he could see us inside. There wasn't any chance to stop the car but he at least knew what he was looking for. Otherwise, he said, the wire had worked perfectly and everything Harvey had said was on the record. After we pulled out of the garage, he ordered up the police helicopter and got on our trail. They couldn't tell from my clues where, exactly, we had stopped the car, but with the aid of a map and some time/speed/distance calculations, they zeroed in on the gravel pit.

I gave them a full statement of everything I knew, or suspected, about Harvey's role in the embezzlement, the murders of Susannah Townsend and Ann Conway, and his relationships with Elliot Lamey and Steve Randall. It seemed clear that Lamey would be indicted for the break-in at my home. Randall was another matter. The evidence against him wasn't conclusive, but Ray thought it likely that Lamey would sell out Randall if it might get him a lighter sentence.

The charges against Albert Bullard would be dismissed, and the department would conduct a full review of the handling of the investigation that led to his arrest, particularly focusing on Randall's role. It seemed likely that, one way or another, Steve Randall's days as our prosecutor were numbered. He'd be lucky to dodge a charge of prosecutorial misconduct. It was difficult to see how he could stay in the mayoral race.

A team of executives and lawyers from Ellis' bank were the next to show up, accompanied by the new lawyer hired by the Tichner family. The lawyer was not from Harvey's firm, I noticed. Ellis had advised the bank president that they needed to talk with me about Harvey's actions as trustee of the XYZ Trust. I described to them what I thought had happened to the funds intended for the symphony. They said that a full review would be conducted with the help of a forensic auditor. I was assured that, if any funds had been diverted from the symphony, they would be restored.

The news media were insistent, calling every half hour for two days, but I refused to give any interviews. They finally gave up. There were screaming headlines about a hostage-taking and the police shooting of a prominent lawyer. But the situation would only be complicated by the mess the media were likely to make of anything I told them. There would be plenty of follow-up stories to pounce on, once the police had finished their work with Elliot Lamey and Steven Randall.

Ted Crawford called. "Ready for a round of golf?" he asked. "I'm not above taking advantage of a wounded man." I laughed. "I could beat you playing with my left arm," I said. "Name the time."

"I'll get back to you," he said. "I don't want you to hurt yourself."

"Thanks for calling," I said. "Stay tuned for further developments in the Townsend case."

"Yeah?" he said. "Listen, promise me a full briefing, when you can. This should be good."

"You're on," I said, and we hung up.

The next call was from Priscilla Freitag. "Hi," she said. "It's Your Girl Friday. You OK?"

"I'm fine, Priscilla," I said. "Thanks again for all your help. I don't think I'd have figured it out without you."

"So Harvey was the thief? And he killed Mrs. Townsend?" she said.

"Yes, and Ann Conway," I said. "But keep that under your hat. The police are still wrapping things up. There'll be more to come."

"Right," she said. "Will do."

"Priscilla," I said. "Congratulations are in order. You've been named this year's winner of the Carrolton Associates Scholarship for Struggling Law Students. It provides full tuition in the day program at the law school, from now until you graduate." There was no such scholarship, until now, but it seemed like a good idea. I figured that the check I was going to get from Morrie in payment for my services would about cover the expense.

"What?" she said.

"You can quit your dishwashing job and go to school full time. We'll fund your tuition."

"What?" she said again.

"And when you graduate, I'd like to talk with you about joining my firm and heading up our intellectual property department."

"You don't have an intellectual property department."

"Not yet," I said. "But think about it."

"Carrolton...," she said. But then she choked up. "Talk to you later," she said, and hung up.

Then Tommy called. "I've been down to police headquarters," he said. "The buzz is all about you and Harvey Anderson. The department is feeling really good about how things turned out, especially if they're not going to have to deal with Steve Randall any more. Chief Matthews is walking around with a big smile on his face. Everybody thinks Ray is some kind of hero for not giving up on the Townsend case. He tells me he has you to thank for breaking the case open. You and your girlfriend. Who I still haven't met, by the way."

I asked him to hold for a minute and talked to Ellis.

"Do you and Jane have any plans for dinner?" I said to Tommy.

"Just a sec," he said, and put down the phone. A minute later he picked back up. "No," he said.

"Then you're coming here, to Ellis' place. Seven o'clock." And I gave him directions.

The dinner was a big success. Tommy was smitten by Ellis, and Jane loved her. As they were leaving, Tommy pulled me aside.

"Nice going," he said. "I'm proud of you."

It was now early evening and Ellis and I were sitting on a swing on the porch of the Michigan cottage, rocking back and forth in small arcs. The catboat bobbed at its mooring just off the end of the dock, in the light west wind. I had grilled a steak for dinner and Ellis cooked corn on the cob. The sun had set but enough light remained to make out the contours of the lakeshore and the tree line above it. The moon was rising in the east and, in the west, heavy clouds were gathering. The forecast was for rain tonight and colder temperatures tomorrow. Indian summer couldn't last forever.

"Are you happy?" I asked.

"Very happy," she said. She was quiet for a moment.

"I really haven't thanked you," she said.

"For what?"

"For saving my life. You jumped in front of me. Harvey shot…. You could have been killed. I don't think I could have lived with…." She broke down and cried.

I put my arm around her – the good arm – and she sobbed into my shoulder for a couple of minutes. It was overdue. This was her first release of emotion since that day in the gravel pit. I stroked her hair. She eventually recovered and dried her eyes.

"I love you too," I said. "Let's go to bed."

Ellis broke into a smile. "Aye, aye, skipper," she said.

Author's Note

This book was an experiment. I enjoy the crime novel genre and I wanted to see if I could write one. Imagine my surprise when, about one year later, I found that I had done so. Not to suggest that the result of my effort is deserving of shelf space alongside works of those authors whose books I have admired. I have a whole new appreciation for the talent and industry required to create a story with complex characters and a multifaceted plot. It was difficult enough to construct this modest tale.

But it was great fun, too. It is true, as they say, that the characters take over the book. I could hardly wait to see what happened next.

A few disclaimers may be in order. This story has no basis in fact. It is only the product of my imagination. I have never served on the board of directors or otherwise been involved in the operations of a symphony orchestra, and none of the organizations I have served was the victim of embezzlement. The setting could be any large Midwestern city. Any resemblance that the plot elements or the characters may have to real situations or persons is coincidental and unintended.

My thanks, as always, to my wife, Nancy, for her encouragement and support. It was a special treat to meet Steve Hamilton, one of my favorite storytellers, at a bookstore in Charlevoix last summer, and he was kind enough to offer his advice and encouragement. I also am indebted to Rick Beard, Marcia and Mike Hittle and Katie and Len Betley for reading drafts of the book and making many valuable comments. Special thanks to my editor, Kathie Snedeker, for her careful review of the manuscript and her insightful suggestions. The end result is, of course, my sole responsibility.

I hope that you enjoyed reading this book as much as I enjoyed writing it.

Berkley Duck
Leland, Michigan
November, 2012